DEATH COMES

by Char

My earliest memories are of an idyllic village in Wensleydale, next to the river Ure, a safe reassuring world for a small child, a world long gone. Over the years I have enjoyed walking in the Yorkshire Dales, especially in Wharfedale where the Buckden-Cray-Hubberholme Triangle Walk is particularly enjoyable. But, what if, above the isolated hamlet of Cray, there was a cottage, and within that cottage was a very dangerous individual indeed? From such an idea comes this work of fiction!

And so it begins….

FIVE YEARS EARLIER

It was a crisp autumnal morning when three ordinary-looking men stopped on the pavement outside a small Edwardian property in Hampstead. Its square front garden was unkempt grass, with a three-foot-high white brick boundary wall and a narrow entrance with no gate. One man appeared to be giving instructions to the other two, or so thought the driver in the car parked opposite. They walked purposefully down the concrete path to the front door where one of them said something into the microphone in the brickwork. The door opened automatically. The two subordinates, each with his right hand readied in his jacket pocket, crossed the hallway and went through a door followed closely by the other man. The room that they entered was windowless, stark, with a desk and two chairs, lit only by a single light bulb. Standing in front of the desk was a fifty-year-old man, hard looking, dressed in dark colours, holding an automatic pistol in front of him in a two-handed grip. Behind him, to the side, was a much younger man, softer looking, handsome, with a double-edged bladed knife raised in his right hand. Before the first two men entering the room had any time to react, the older man squeezed the trigger of his gun, re-adjusted instantly, and squeezed it again. The third man reached to his left shoulder, inside his jacket, as the young man's knife speeded through the air and buried itself in the door jamb an inch from his neck.

1

The older man re-adjusted his aim once more, but the third man was already out of the door as a bullet smacked into a wall behind him. Outside, in the parked car, the driver saw a man running for his life down the path and out into the street. He crossed the road behind the car and was gone. In the house, the older man stood above two dead bodies lying on the floor and smiled.

'They shouldn't have tried that. So unwise,' said the younger man.

'Yes,' replied the older man. 'But it's time for us to disappear.'

The two men walked calmly out of the house, crossed the road and got into the parked car.

'What the hell happened in there!' asked the driver.

'Pre-cognitive self-defence,' laughed the younger man.

'Drive!' exclaimed the older.

SATURDAY THE FIRST WEEK IN JULY

'Good question, Mrs T, not sure yet but I think I'll cycle up to Hubberholme and then walk the triangle. It's supposed to stay sunny all day, with maybe a shower or two. I should be back by six-ish so an evening meal would be good, if that's OK?'

Mrs Taylor, owner of a bed and breakfast in Kettlewell, smiled at the handsome young student. She'd retired to Wharfedale some ten years ago and, with no family to speak of, ran her guest house primarily for company and to keep herself busy. Andrew Wilson was one of her regulars.

'Fine, Andrew. Steak and kidney pie?'

'Excellent, Mrs T,' said the young Leeds University student.

He glanced at his watch. It was just coming up to eight o'clock.

With a cheery wave and a 'see you later' he got on his bicycle and turned left out of the drive onto the narrow country road to head up the dale. It was mid-summer. He felt exhilarated to be on his summer vac, out of the city and in such glorious countryside. He whistled as he pedalled along, glancing up at the green hillsides strewn with sheep. Every now and then he was overtaken by a car going too fast, some local on the way to work, and only just avoided a head on collision with an inattentive farmer on a tractor coming the other way. He made good time on his road bike and, after turning off the main road at Buckden, arrived in the small hamlet of Hubberholme well before nine. He got off the bike and lent it against a graveyard wall opposite a white walled pub, The George. He studiously looked across at the squat Norman church and tried to recall the name of the famous writer who he thought had been buried there, but it wouldn't come. He took off his backpack and looked inside for his map of the Triangle Walk. It wasn't there.

'Bugger,' he muttered to himself. Yes, it was still on the bedside table. Oh well, he'd use his phone and GPS. He had a rough idea of the route and it was only six or seven miles. Hard to get lost, surely?

He half hid his bike on the other side of the wall, being sure that no-one would steal it anyway in these parts. He set off on foot along an obvious path and stopped just beyond the church to consult his mobile. The signal was weak and the cheap smartphone was struggling. It currently told him that he was in Buckden, which was over a mile away. He committed his route to memory as best he could. A limestone crag towered above him a good distance away to his right and he headed left along a winding farm track that provided an easier climb. The track crossed a wide hedgeless grass field, almost a meadow, inhabited by black and white Friesian cows who stared at him dismissively as they chewed their cud.

4

At the top of the field was a rather impressive stone farmhouse that must have been at least two hundred years old. He strode into the concreted farmyard, becoming unnecessarily nervous as a border collie ran towards him, barking before sitting before him proud, as if on guard. He ruffled the dog's coat and patted it with a 'good boy'.

'It's a bitch,' laughed the farmer, appearing out of nowhere. 'Know where you're going, young man?'

'Yes, fine thanks. I'm doing the triangle walk,' the student replied.

'The wrong way around,' added the wiser of the two.

Andrew feigned a laugh, slightly puzzled, and headed off right, along a marked public footpath.

'Stay left up the hill,' shouted the farmer, but his words fell on deaf ears.

Twenty minutes later, after following the path through an old wood, Andrew found himself at the bottom of the limestone crag with no obvious way up. He considered going back and asking the farmer, but no, he was twenty-two. Twenty-two-year olds can look after themselves. He consulted his phone. No signal here! He decided to scramble up the side of the crag. Halfway up he stopped to rest and eat a bar of chocolate while he surveyed Wharfedale set out before him in all its splendour. In the distance he could see the dale widening out, and he spotted a campsite by the river, with a group of children splashing about. Over to his left, a few miles off now, he could see the hillside disappearing into cloud above Buckden. 'That must be the Pike,' he mused. Directly above him, a hundred feet in the air, he saw a buzzard slowly circling. His spirits soared and, renewed by chocolate, he turned to continue his climb. He soon reached the top and stood gazing around. The grass was sparser here and was dotted about with small limestone rocks, like deliberately strewn debris. There was no sign of a footpath now and he couldn't get his GPS to work. Nevertheless, from memory he knew he had to go right. So long as he found the terrace walk along the top of the scar, that led to paths down to Cray, he'd be OK. After ten minutes or so, he came across an obvious track to his left, going higher. He decided to follow it. 'It must go somewhere,' he thought, laughing to himself. It did. As he came over the brow of a hill, in front of him, only two hundred yards away, he could see a small stone cottage and a couple of farm buildings. Beyond it was a tarmac lane and, set way down in the valley, maybe a mile or two off, he could make out a small village. 'That must be Cray,' he thought.

It was then that he was startled by the sound of a gunshot that broke the silence of the country air. He was certain it came from inside the cottage. Or did it? It didn't sound like a shotgun. And there was no echo. More like a pistol. He stood completely still and listened intently. Not a sound, and he could see no-one around outside. He stared at the cottage windows and thought he saw movement. He felt suddenly frightened and then stupid. This was Wharfedale after all, but his instinct was fear, and flight. He circled around the cottage, keeping his distance, his eyes fixed on the windows, and quickly made it to the tarmac lane. He began to laugh.

'What an idiot you are, Andy! Just a farmer having a pop at a rabbit, I should think.'

His mood lightened but, nevertheless, he jogged to the end of the lane before turning left onto a road that provided him with a gentle walk down into Cray. There, he stopped outside the Lion to take stock of his route, before crossing the main road and climbing slowly a few hundred feet to the Buckden Pike footpath. The climb to the summit of the Pike would be for another day. Instead, he headed down the track on the hillside above the main road and eventually reached The Inn at Buckden, a small welcoming white-walled pub. He got himself a pint of John Smiths and sat in a corner, on his own, people watching. It was lunchtime and the bar was almost full, with a mixture of a few locals and tourist families enjoying pub grub. He was mulling over his more than eventful walk when he was distracted by the extremely attractive bar maid serving drinks. She was blonde, looked mid-twenties, and had a figure to die for. The barman was about forty and ordinary looking, sounded local from his Yorkshire accent, and was very chatty with his customers. 'Probably her husband,' he thought, although they didn't look like a natural pairing. 'She looks more like a film star than a bar maid,' Andrew

Wilson said to himself as he finished his pint. He sat a while and then picked up his backpack and left the pub. Outside, he stood and stared across at the limestone crag two miles away. Circling above, as if he'd been followed, was that same buzzard again. This time its presence disturbed him and his back suddenly shivered incongruously in the hot summer sun as he crossed the road to walk the last leg back into Hubberholme. The Buckden Triangle was then complete. He retrieved his bike and ate another bar of chocolate.

Three hours later, back in Kettlewell, he had showered and changed his clothes and was sitting across the table from Mrs Taylor, enjoying his steak and kidney pie, chips and peas, telling her all about his day.

He told her about the cottage and the gunshot.

She laughed.

'Probably just a farmer taking a pot shot at a pheasant,' she offered.

'Yes, probably,' he replied, unsmilingly, but the Buckden Triangle walk had left Andrew Wilson with a distinct feeling of unease.

Just before lunchtime, at The Inn in Buckden, a phone conversation had taken place.

'Don't shout at me, Sal, it wasn't like that. He wasn't just a walker, he recognized me, I'm sure. Anyway, it's happened. I'll move the body tonight. It might just be a coincidence that he turned up at the pub first, it's an obvious place to stay, but there's a chance he knew who you were. You must get rid of his stuff. Check it over first and then clear his room. Did he come by car?'

'I booked him in, he seemed ordinary to me, a bit curious maybe. There's no sign of a car, I've checked the car park out back. He probably got a bus here. Hell, Jonny! I'll sort the room out and burn his stuff. Don't worry, just get rid of the body.'

'Good girl. I'll dump it miles away. I'll phone you when I get back, but it'll be late. Love you.'

'Take care, Jonny. I'd better get back to the bar.'

Hours later, as the mid-summer sun was at last setting, he zipped his phone in his bomber jacket pocket and looked down at the still body in the middle of the grey stone kitchen floor for what seemed like the thousandth time. He'd made up his mind what to do. Over the moor would be best but it could take half the night. He decided to wrap the body just in case he came across any late walkers. He went out the back to the dilapidated farm building with its rusty tin sheeting roof and found a couple of blue plastic feed bags and some billy-band that had been in there for more than twenty years. Back in the cottage he tied the man's legs and arms together and then put the lower and upper halves of the body in the two bags, before tying lengths of the red string around the gruesome parcel. Although of small stature, and thin as a lath, he was a strong fit man, still in his twenties, and had no trouble lifting the body. He carried it outside and draped it over the back of his quadbike, securing it with more string. It was after ten o'clock now and, with a full moon, it was lighter than he'd wanted. As well as the body, he took a small can of petrol and his shotgun with him as he noisily set off up the path that led to the crag. Luck was on his side. He saw no-one and, more importantly, no-one saw him. After a mile he turned off the path and onto the moor.

He had to take great care now. It would be so easy to turn the quadbike over. The moonlight was key. He could see well enough, and knew the area, but he reckoned that he needed to put at least five miles between the cottage and where the body would be found, as surely it would be, eventually. Where he could, he used criss-crossing public footpaths, avoiding roads, and was heading generally south. He made slow progress until, at last, he came to Mastiles Lane above Kilnsey. This was a centuries old drovers' road, well used these days by walkers and bikers, and even off-roaders, with dry stone walls on either side for much of its length. He felt confident now and speeded up, covering another mile or so. He was well and truly in the middle of nowhere, a good place to be.

With no sign of a gate, or a stile, or a footpath, nearby, he brought the quadbike to a halt and switched it off. He stood in the middle of the lane and listened. He could hear nothing. Absolute silence. It was well after midnight now and the sky was a stargazer's dream. He smiled to himself. Then, his mind focussing on the job in hand, he manhandled the plastic parcel to lean it against a dry stone wall to his left. He scrambled up the wall and carefully dragged the parcel over the top, the body hurtling to the ground on the other side. He got down off the wall and picked up the can of petrol and his shotgun, and then got back over the wall. He removed the billy-band and the two blue plastic bags and tossed them back over the wall next to the quadbike. He then re-checked that, before leaving the cottage, he'd taken everything from the man's pockets, and his watch. As dead eyes stared up at him, after loading the shotgun, he put its barrel against the man's mouth and pulled the trigger. The face was obliterated as the gun shot echoed around the empty moor. He swore to himself as he realized he was spattered with blood. He was angry and kicked out at the lifeless body. He unscrewed the cap on the can and dowsed the body in petrol. Estimating that there was no living soul within two miles, he lit a match and gently lobbed it onto the body. The fire was, initially, fierce and he jumped back.

'Try identifying that!' he said, laughing to himself.

He was surprised at how quickly the flames died. He climbed back over the wall, picked up the two plastic bags and put them behind the seat of the quadbike. Belatedly, he wiped drying blood from his hands with a cloth. He took one final look over the wall at the body, now barely smouldering, and got on the quadbike. He checked his phone but there was no signal. It was after one o'clock and it was a long way back. He decided to take the shorter route home, back along Mastiles Lane to Kilnsey Crag, and then up the main road through Kettlewell. He made good time. Several cars overtook him, and one car honked its horn at an idiot on a quadbike with poor lights on a main road in the middle of the night. He turned off the road after Buckden and climbed the steep hill above Cray. At around two o'clock he switched off the quadbike after parking it inside the farm building. He was shattered and couldn't face a phone call grilling. Instead, he texted.

'Back. Everything fine.'

SUNDAY THE FIRST WEEK IN JULY

It was a sunny still Sunday morning, the day after terrible events had come to the peaceful Yorkshire dale. Sally Henshaw woke up suddenly in her single bed, having slept fitfully. The text from her brother had been short and not sweet. She was desperate to know exactly what had happened up there at the cottage. She'd done her bit as Jonny had told her to. Room 2 had been cleared and, after learning no more about her guest, she'd burned all his effects in the incinerator. Her husband Tom, landlord of The Inn, had been busy all the previous evening in the bar, serving a bunch of alcoholics from a Leeds walking club, and had no idea of what his wife had been doing. At around seven o'clock that morning he knocked gently on the bedroom door and walked in carrying a cup of tea. He seemed in a good mood.

'Morning, Sal. What did you get up to last night? I could have done with more help in the bar. Katy and I were run off our feet with a load of lads from Leeds. I've booked them in to the chalet. They're heading up Whernside today, then back here for the night. Good trade, they drink like fish and want a big breakfast.'

She didn't answer his question and just sipped on her tea.

'Does our guest in Room 2, Mister Wilson isn't it, want a full English, do you know?'

The shock of the question made her spill the tea. She looked nervously back at her husband, mopping the duvet with a tissue from under her pillow.

'Oh, Mister Wilson left yesterday, early evening. He'd got to get back to Skipton, I think. Something about a phone call. He must have caught the last bus.'

'Caught the last bus! Why would he get the bus?' came the reply from her puzzled husband.

'Why wouldn't he get the bus?' she shouted back.

'Because his bloody sports car is in our garage, that's why! What the hell's going on?'

Peter Wilson had driven up from Skipton in his 1959 Austin Healey Sprite very early on Saturday morning, enjoying a ride out in his classic car, just for fun, or so it had seemed. He'd pulled into the car park at the rear of the pub and met Tom Henshaw, who was about to set up the food board by the side of the road. He'd told Tom that he'd like to book in for bed and breakfast, just for one night, and was going to do the Triangle Walk, but he was concerned about his car if it happened to rain. The Sprite had no soft top. Tom had offered his own garage for the day since his car and landrover always stood out in the pub car park anyway.

'I thought he came by bus. I'm sure that's what he told me,' said Sally. 'He checked out about six. Maybe he forgot his car.'

'Don't be bloody stupid, woman! Well, very strange. You don't know anything else?'

'No, Tom. Maybe he was going to walk somewhere else up here but didn't want to say. Best leave the car where it is. No doubt he'll be back for it.'

'OK, I suppose you're right. Sorry for shouting, Sal. I'll just leave it in the garage. It'll take no harm.'

With that, he bent over her and gave her a peck on the cheek. He took her empty cup and left the room, off to prepare ten breakfasts for the walkers.

Sally Henshaw lay there staring at the ceiling, thoughts churning, feeling sick. What should she do? She'd better go up to the cottage when she could get away and try to sort things out. She needed to know more. How had Peter Wilson ended up dead? And that car? It would have to disappear.

At about the same time, Andrew Wilson was tucking into one of Mrs Taylor's special Sunday breakfasts. An hour later he was overly full, on his bike, heading lazily down the road to Skipton. He'd enjoyed the Triangle Walk. It had been as good as everyone said, and he laughed to himself as he put his 'bit of excitement' into perspective. He got back to his parents' by about eleven. Mrs T's full

English followed by his mum's Sunday lunch, what a good day food-wise! So much better than his own student food in his Leeds University flat. He wasn't much good at self-catering and loved his mum's home cooking during his summer break from studies.

He leant his bike against the garage door and walked straight into the bungalow. His dad was reading the Sunday paper. He looked up and nodded, a man of few words. Andrew nodded back and went through into the kitchen where his mother was basting a beef joint before putting it back into the oven.

'Dinner will be ready in about an hour, young man. Did you enjoy your trip? Mrs Taylor spoil you as usual?'

Andrew kissed his mother on the cheek.

'Yes, of course she spoiled me. She thinks of me as a nephew, I reckon. I walked the Hubberholme-Cray-Buckden triangle yesterday. Great views, mam, and smashing sunshine. Uncle Peter would love it, though he's probably done it years ago.'

'Well, it's funny you say that. You didn't come across him then?'

'No, why?'

'Well, he rang just after you left on Friday and I told him what you were up to. He said he was going to have a ride out in that little car of his on Saturday. Might go up the

16

dale and over to Hawes to buy cheese at the cheese factory. Or, since you were doing the triangle, he said he might stop somewhere and do it himself. He thought you'd get a big surprise if you came across him. He must have decided not to bother.'

'Yes, I suppose so. That's a pity though. We could have had a pint or two. I'll give him a ring later.'

'That would be nice, dear. He said he'd bring me a selection of cheeses if he got to Hawes.'

They both laughed.

It was mid-afternoon when Sally Henshaw managed to get away from the bar at The Inn, after the Sunday lunch rush had calmed down and Tom could cope, with help from Katy and Rita, two local girls who worked part-time at the pub when needs must. She checked the small blue sportscar in the garage. There was no sign of the ignition key, and it certainly hadn't been left in Peter Wilson's room. She popped her head through the side entrance to the bar and shouted across at her husband:

'Just off up to see mum for a couple of hours. I'll make tea when I get back.'

And with that, she was gone, with no chance of a reply. She got in the landrover and set off for Cray, barely two miles further up the dale. She turned left and climbed a winding road in the direction of the crag and then right, down the tarmac farm track to Scargill Cottage. As she slammed the landrover door shut she saw a face at the kitchen window. She waved in her usual way and walked down the path into the cottage. The small figure on the couch looked up fearfully, eyes staring.

'Well, mother, you must know what happened, why it happened, how it happened! I need to speak to Jonny.'

'You can't,' came the curt reply.

'Why not? I need to find things out. This wasn't supposed to happen!'

'You can't see him. He's very tired and upset. You can only talk to me today.'

She was obstinate. Sally looked to the ceiling and muttered an expletive to herself.

'Alright mother. So, did a man come here yesterday morning, and did he see Jonny, and did Jonny kill him, mother?'

'Yes, Jonny killed him.'

'How?'

'He shot him.'

'What with?'

'With a pistol.'

'He doesn't have a pistol, mother.'

'Maybe he got one. Or maybe he didn't shoot him.'

Sally lifted her head and swore at the ceiling again.

'Have you been making sure that Jonny is alright, mother?'

'Yes, I have.'

'Has Jonny been taking his tablets, mother?'

'Jonny didn't want them last week. He wanted not to take them.'

'Good grief! You know that Jonny needs his pills. Otherwise, things can happen.'

Sally's eyes were burrowing into mother's head now. Mother started to cry.

'I'm sorry, Sally, but Jonny got rid of the body. Everything is alright now, isn't it?'

Sally shook her head.

'No, mother. That man was Mister Wilson. He was staying at the pub and he had a car. I got rid of his clothes and his bags, and I told Tom that he'd left, but Tom is suspicious. I must get rid of the car before people turn up looking for Mister Wilson, but I don't have the car key.'

Mother smiled.

'Oh, that's easy. After Jonny cleaned up, he put the man's keys, with his watch and his phone and his wallet, in the kitchen drawer. So now you've got his car keys, everything is alright?'

Sally sighed.

'Yes, everything is alright.'

She went into the kitchen and found Peter Wilson's keys in the drawer, including a small key with a Healey badge attached. She went through his wallet but found nothing useful, just cash and a credit card. His watch and mobile phone were smashed, as if they had been stamped on. She decided to leave further discussion of yesterday's events until she could talk to Jonny. She made a pot of tea and returned to mother. After spending another hour just quietly talking, she left the cottage and hurried back to The Inn and a non-too-pleased husband.

Also, that same afternoon, Andrew Wilson cycled the half mile to his uncle's house to tell him about his Triangle walk, and maybe get the cheese for his mother. The house was locked and, though a small hatchback stood on the drive, there was no sign of the blue Sprite, and no sign of his uncle. As Andrew set off back home, he knew he was starting to worry. Uncle Peter was a very organized man. If he was expected back by now, he should be back. When

Andrew got home, he tried ringing his uncle's mobile phone, but got no reply.

MONDAY THE FIRST WEEK IN JULY

On Monday morning, Tom Henshaw headed off to Skipton in the landrover to buy stock for the bar. He had said that he had a few other things to do and that he probably wouldn't get back 'til mid-afternoon. The pub didn't open 'til six. Sally decided to seize her opportunity, to move the sportscar which was still in their garage. The idea was to get it far enough away but be able to get back to The Inn before her husband. Tom had gone south. Sally turned right out of the pub car park and headed north up the dale in the Sprite. The tiny open-top Healey was unlike any car she'd driven before. It seemed twitchy and she crawled up the hairpin bends that led over the top of Wharfedale and down into Wensleydale. On reaching the A684 she turned left and, a few miles later, found herself moving at snail's pace through the cobbled street into the market town of Hawes. The tiny classic car, driven by a golden-haired young woman, stuck out like a sore thumb. At the end of the main street, she followed a sign to a small public car park, where she parked in a corner, near obscuring bushes. She got out of the car, leaving the key in the ignition.

'I hope someone steals the bloody thing and drives it to the coast,' she thought to herself.

She was shaking with nerves now and realised that this had been a bad idea. Nevertheless, the car was a long way from the pub, and a long way from the dead body lying up on

Mastiles Lane. She now had to get home. It had only taken her forty-five minutes to get here but buses didn't go to Buckden by the route she'd come. They went west and down Ribblesdale to Skipton where she'd have to get another bus back up to Buckden. She left the car park and walked down the main street searching for the right bus stop. For a second, she thought of a taxi but knew that was too dangerous.

Early that Monday morning, Andrew Wilson had tried ringing Uncle Peter, several times. His mum had started to worry too. It was so unlike her brother-in-law. They drove round to his house but there was no sign of life.

'What should we do, mum? It's just not like him. He should be back by now and he would've rung if he'd had bother with the Sprite. Maybe he's been taken ill or crashed or something.'

Andrew was trying to stay calm, and failing.

'But the police would have rung us if something bad had happened. Maybe he's phoned his neighbours, he gets on well with Mister Jackson next door.'

They tried Mister Jackson, and a couple of other houses nearby but no-one had seen Peter Wilson, or the blue Sprite, since before the weekend.

Andrew's mum had a thought.

'Supposing he didn't do the Triangle. You never saw him, after all. Supposing he did go over to Hawes, to the cheese factory, like he said he might. He might have decided to stay a couple of nights, maybe have a walk or two over there.'

'Well, I can't stand us doing nothing,' said Andrew. 'Let's go to Hawes and see if we can spot him. There aren't many Sprites about, that's for sure!'

The mother and son set off up Wharfedale, passing through Buckden, tracing out Sally Henshaw's route to Hawes, about thirty minutes behind her. They both knew Hawes well and were frequent visitors to the cheese factory. They'd try there first. As Andrew drove slowly into the market town, along the main street, he glanced automatically to his left, his eyes diverted by a stunning blonde waiting at a bus stop. He recognised her instantly. Once seen, never forgotten.

Two minutes later, as Sally Henshaw got on the bus to Skipton, Andrew and his mother turned into the local car park and parked against the wall at the top end.

'I'll get a two-hour ticket mum, then we can walk up to the cheese factory.'

'No need, son, look over there, in the opposite corner, next to those bushes.'

They got out of the car and stood stock still, staring at the blue Sprite. Andrew ran over to the sports car and

24

immediately removed the key from the ignition, holding it high above his head.

'I don't like this, mum. Where is Uncle Peter? He'd never leave the car with its key in. I've got bad feelings about this. What should we do?'

'Don't panic. There'll be an explanation, but we don't know what it is. Have you got a photo of Uncle Peter on your phone?'

'Brilliant, mum. Let's try the cheese factory. He must've gone there. We can try pubs and hotels. Someone will have seen him.'

Andrew's mood lifted. They had a plan, but his mum felt scared.

The bus from Hawes got into Skipton at 1.30. It had made good time. Sally walked quickly out of the bus station and found the bus stop for Buckden, half-way up the high street. As she climbed onto the bus, seated outside the pub opposite, sipping on a pint of John Smiths, was her husband. Tom Henshaw stared across at her in disbelief.

As the bus set off, he whispered to himself, 'What the hell are you doing here, Sally girl?'

By about four o'clock, Andrew and his mother had shown Peter Wilson's photograph to staff in the cheese factory and had been up and down Hawes main street twice. They must have asked more than fifty people if they'd seen him. No-one had recognised him for definite, although at least three did say that they might have. Andrew had also shown a photo of his uncle's pride and joy, the blue Austin Healey Sprite, with its owner sat in the driver's seat, smiling at the camera, but with no luck. The two of them were tired now, and Andrew's mother was becoming increasingly upset. Sitting outside a tea shop, having a strong coffee and a well-earned bacon butty, was a young police officer. They approached the policeman. Mrs Wilson blurted out the events of their day and their worries about her brother-in-law. The officer placated them, smiled, and studied a photograph. No, he hadn't seen him, but when he was presented with a second photo, of Peter Wilson in the Sprite, his face changed. The smile was gone. He remembered seeing a blue sportscar that morning, certainly very like the Sprite, but thought that the driver had been a woman.

'Your brother-in-law doesn't have a lady friend around here?' he asked.

'No, certainly not,' replied Mrs Wilson, glancing at her son.

'It's an unusual car. Let's go check it out,' he suggested.

They walked to the car park and the police officer searched the car and made notes.

'I'm sure there is nothing to worry about, Mrs Wilson but, after all you've told me, I will ring it in as a possible missing person. We'll do some checking around for you, hospital, doctors, etcetera, purely routine, and see what we come up with. As I say, don't you worry. I suggest you go home. I'll get back to you within twenty-four hours. Give Skipton police station a call if your brother-in-law gets in touch.'

On their way back to Skipton, Andrew tried to lift his mother's spirits, but after a few miles, they both fell silent. Without telling each other, both felt certain that something dreadful had happened.

It was later than usual that afternoon when Tom Henshaw got back to The Inn. He unloaded the landrover and re-stocked the bar with bottles of spirits, nibbles, crisps and peanuts, standard fare for the locals. Before opening time, he sat down with his wife to have a swift cup of tea and re-heated chilli con carne.

'Did you have a good day? Get up to much?' he asked in a matter of fact way.

'No, not much. Tidied round. Got the evening menu sorted with Katy. Oh, and Mister Wilson returned for his sportscar,' Sally offered, keeping her eyes looking down at her plate.

'That's good,' he continued, 'when did he turn up?'

'This afternoon. Must've been visiting a friend nearby.'

'Really,' said her husband, the tone of his voice changing. 'What time was he here then?'

Sally recognised suspicion in her husband's voice and thought quickly.

'He turned up just after I got back from Skipton. I finished my chores early and thought I'd join you for lunch. Never came across you though. Forgot my phone, too, would you believe?

'And used the bus,' he added, with a note of finality.

Their eating continued in silence.

That evening, Andrew Wilson sat with his mother and father discussing the day's events. Andrew's dad still didn't think there was anything to worry about.

'He was always a bit mysterious, you know, when he was working down in London, before he packed in and came back up here to Skipton. Too bright for his own good.'

Andrew thought that was a very odd thing to say but didn't question it. His mum looked annoyed.

'Well, we're worried, Jack. And that policeman in Hawes, he certainly took us seriously.'

At that very moment, a car pulled up outside. Two men got out and walked down the drive to the front door. One was the police officer they'd talked to earlier. The other man was older, besuited, and was obviously a senior officer of some sort. Andrew answered the door and showed them through to the small living room. They seemed relaxed and seated themselves on the couch, next to Andrew. The young police officer started the conversation, addressing all three of the Wilson family, who were looking very fearful.

'I am PC Craven, of the Skipton police and this is Mr Tanner. We have no news to update you on about Peter Wilson.'

There was an audible sigh of relief.

'He has been designated formally as missing and we are going through all possible channels to ascertain his whereabouts. Request for help from local media will not be sought at this time, but perhaps in a day or two, depending on what develops. I've brought along Mr Tanner who would like to ask you all a few questions.'

'Hang on a minute, young man,' said Andrew's father tersely, 'but who exactly are you, Mr Tanner? I don't reckon you're a policeman. Am I right?'

David Tanner smiled.

'You are indeed correct, Mr Wilson. For the purposes of our conversation, shall we just say that I work for the government authorities, Special Branch if you wish?'

With this, he removed a small brown leather wallet from his jacket and flashed an identification card all too fleetingly.

'What's going on here?' queried Andrew. 'I don't understand. What's Uncle Peter got to do with you?'

'What do you really know about Peter and his working life?' asked Tanner.

'I'd better answer that,' interjected Andrew's father. 'Jean and Andy know nothing really. All I know is that my brother worked throughout his career for the government. He told everybody he was a civil servant working in London, but I knew there was more to it than that, from little bits of things he said to me over the years. I'm guessing he was like you, eh, Mister Tanner?'

'He wasn't just like me, Mr Wilson, he has been a colleague of mine for more than ten years. When he retired and came back here to Skipton, it wasn't just to enjoy a quiet life in Wharfedale, and to tinker about with that beloved Sprite of his. He has been working, sort of unofficially, but I can't say more than that. What I need is for you to tell me anything you know about what Peter has been doing, or where he's been, or who he's seen, in the last month or so. Anything out of the ordinary?'

'Bloody hell,' said Jack Wilson, putting his hands to his forehead. His wife's face emphasised her shock. Andrew hugged her and then went through to the kitchen to make them all a pot of tea. It would be a long evening.

There followed nearly two hours of questions from Tanner, with police officer Mark Craven making copious notes, useful interjections and trying to keep the family upbeat and positive about Peter Wilson. Craven was vital to Tanner. He knew the local area in detail. Eventually the interview, for that is what the conversation had become, came to the events of the last few days and, in particular, the previous Friday, the day before Peter Wilson had gone for his run-out in the Sprite.

'Peter rang in the morning to say that he was having a weekend jaunt in that car of his. It was getting serviced at Tony's Garage that day 'to make sure that it's spot on', I remember him saying.'

Jean Wilson's words triggered the same thought immediately in Tanner and Craven's minds.

'Mileage!' they both said at the same time.

At midnight, David Tanner, an officer in the British Secret Service, shook hands with the Wilson family and told them not to worry.

On the way to Skipton police station, where the Sprite was now situated, he suggested to officer Craven that, because of his local expertise, they should work together. He would square it with his superiors. Craven was pleased, nervous and somewhat overwhelmed. Nothing like this had ever happened in the six years he had been a police constable in sleepy Wharfedale.

Back at the police station, Craven searched the Sprite rigorously once more and, underneath the driver's seat, came across a garage invoice dated the previous Friday. The mileage on the car was 79676 miles. The mileage on the invoice was 79602 miles. The Sprite had, they knew, set off from Peter Wilson's house in Skipton on the Saturday morning and ended up in a car park in Hawes. It had then been driven back to Skipton police station. The obvious route from Skipton to Hawes was about 36 miles, straight up Wharfedale. It looked as though the Sprite had been nowhere else!

TUESDAY THE FIRST WEEK IN JULY

It wasn't until around midday on Tuesday, after a very late night, followed by a good six hours sleep, that David Tanner entered Superintendent Blair's office. The two men shook hands and Blair sat casually glancing out of the window at two jackdaws chasing each other around the lawn outside. After what seemed an age to Tanner, he turned and said:

'Well, Mister Tanner, we've checked you out as best we could. It's always a bit difficult with you secretive types, but you're definitely who you claim to be, even if your name might be somewhat open to debate.'

Tanner smiled and shrugged his shoulders.

'I know that you'll be unwilling to say much, even to a superintendent of police. But let's try one question. Peter Wilson was deemed by his family, and by a junior police officer, to be possibly missing, at around 4 o'clock yesterday afternoon. At 6 o'clock, we here at Skipton had decided to designate him as officially missing. You turned up less than two hours later to flash that card of yours, getting me to make a phone call to London, and finding young Craven to go with you to question the Wilson family. It's a long way from Skipton to anywhere, Mister Tanner. How come you got here so quickly, even if Peter Wilson is an ex-colleague?'

Tanner smiled again.

'Excellent, sir,' he replied. 'Perhaps I haven't been totally frank. In my profession, no-one fully retires. Peter Wilson returned to his native Yorkshire a year ago. His retirement, if I call it such, suited him and us at the time. I can't tell you much more, except to say that for the past year he has been searching for someone, and so have I. The person we seek is hiding somewhere here in the Dales, but as you know, the Dales is a huge area. Peter is based in the south. Me? Further north. As soon as I knew that he was missing, I got here as fast as I could. The man we're after is very dangerous, in all respects.'

'Thank you for that, Mister Tanner. As soon as you knew, eh? Sometimes I worry about what communications you lot are monitoring these days! Do you wish me to treat this as a normal missing person case? Radio, television, the press?'

'No, sir. I fear it would do no good. The fact that Peter Wilson has not been in touch with me for over a week means that he is probably dead.'

The straightforwardness and starkness of Tanner's words shook the superintendent. Tanner continued.

'However, if we do assume the worst, without causing alarm or alerting the press, it would be helpful if you could give resources to searching the area for him. Peter Wilson probably travelled in his sportscar straight up Wharfedale and over to Hawes, where his car was found.'

Blair bit his lip and moved his head slowly from side to side.

'I'll do what I can. I understand you'd like young Craven to help you. He's a bright lad, very keen and he knows the area extremely well. He was brought up in Wharfedale. Would you prefer uniform or plain clothes?'

'Oh, uniform,' replied Tanner. 'More gravitas for the locals.'

He smiled and shook hands once again with Blair. Leaving the office, he looked across at PC Mark Craven sat waiting patiently. The young officer stood immediately.

'OK, officer. You're on. Let's go.'

In the Wilson house, Andrew hadn't yet got out of bed. He'd lain all morning thinking about Uncle Peter, a man he thought he knew well, a dull man some would say, but a nice man who had always been kind to him as a young boy growing up. He was scared for him. The previous evening's questions had produced very few answers for the family, and he'd found Tanner very difficult to like, or trust. He thought that he should do something himself but had no idea what. He was churning everything through his mind when his mother called him down for lunch.

It was also lunchtime for the Henshaws at The Inn in Buckden. The pub didn't open 'til 2. Locals found the opening hours completely baffling for a pub in Wharfedale in mid-summer. 'Don't they want to make money?' they would question each other. Things had been so different for the past four years, since ownership changed. The pub had been owned and run by Tom Henshaw, taken over from his father a few years earlier. Tom was a very hard worker but wasn't the brightest when it came to money. He was just about to go bankrupt when a young lady who lived somewhere above Cray, and who herself hadn't been long in the dale, bought him out, but took him on as the paid landlord. 'All very strange,' most thought. Their relationship was seen to have blossomed and they'd married very quickly. 'They never seemed lovey dovey,' was the consensus, but, for the locals, it didn't matter. They had their pub to go to, with decent beer and food, even if they couldn't quite be sure of when it opened.

'Do you want to tell me what's going on?' said Tom out of the blue.

'What do you mean?' replied Sally Henshaw.

'Come off it. This business with the car, and Mister Wilson leaving it here for a couple of days. And him then turning up after you'd been, for some unknown reason by bus, to Skipton. Is there something going on? Another fella?'

Sally burst out laughing.

'Good God no!' she cried. 'OK, I'll tell you the truth. I came down to Skipton to give you a treat. I thought we could have lunch and a trip on the canal. You've been working too hard and I know I've been neglecting you of late. I do all the money side of things, but you do all the work! So, I thought I'd give you a surprise, but it went wrong. And as for that car, well, I don't know what happened to it. When I got back it had gone and there was no note or anything. I'm a bit worried about Mister Wilson and I'd even thought of ringing the police. What do you think?'

Tom Henshaw sat back in his chair, smiling at his wife, re-assured.

'Don't you worry, girl. Yes, it might be best if we tell the police.'

WEDNESDAY THE FIRST WEEK IN JULY

Early on Wednesday morning Sally phoned the cottage on her mobile. She was dressed and sitting on the side of her bed. Tom had his own single bed, in the room opposite hers. The phone was answered with silence.

'Hello. Jonny, is that you? Answer me, Jonny. Are you alright?'

'Hello Sal. Yes, I'm alright. Everything is alright now. I'm looking after myself. I had a long talk with mother, and she told me what you said.'

Sally then heard uncontrollable sobbing coming from her brother. Gone was the self-confident voice from their previous phone call, when Jonny was telling her what to do and planning the disposal of a dead body. Now, he sounded like an errant child, seeking consolation.

'Oh, Jonny, my love, stop crying dear. You've taken your pills, and you're keeping busy?'

Her brother's mood immediately lifted.

'Oh yes, Sal. I've been on the internet all night. I've found someone who really likes chess. We've been playing online against each other for hours. He doesn't know who I am, of course. I always do incognito online. But it's good and'

'Jonny, Jonny,' she interrupted, 'I need to talk to you or mother this evening. I'll come over around seven and bring supplies. Make sure you stay indoors today. Soon, people will be searching for Mister Wilson. Have a good think. Why do you believe that he knew you? I'll see you this evening. Bye.'

At that very moment, Tom knocked on the bedroom door and walked in.

'Who was on the phone?' he asked.

'Oh, only mother. She needs some supplies and I said I'd get some and see her this evening.'

'She's lucky to have you at her beck and call. Getting on a bit I suppose.'

'Oh, she's only sixty, but with the arthritis, she can't get about like she could and, frankly, sometimes I think she's getting very forgetful. Losing it, maybe.'

'Anyway, she's lucky and I suppose I am too. You look after everything up there. Then again, I do everything down here at the pub, but I do have a stunning bar maid to help me, at least sometimes!'

She smiled, and he laughed, adding in a much more serious voice:

'By the way, it took me ages to get off to sleep last night. I couldn't stop thinking about Mister Wilson and his sportscar. I'm going to go into Skipton this morning and tell the police. It's so strange. Don't worry though, I won't mention you. It was me who said he could put it in the garage. I hope it was him who took it. It must have been, or an opportunist thief. No, that doesn't make sense.'

'Well,' said Sally, 'you don't have to mention that it was in our garage. Why would it be? It could have just been in the pub car park. He disappeared, then his car did, so to speak.'

'An odd way of putting it,' Tom continued, 'but simpler, and it makes no difference to the police.'

Sally smiled again and beckoned him towards the bed.

Later that morning a weary-with-the-world desk sergeant took down details of Peter Wilson's short stay at The Inn, and the facts that Wilson had checked out on Saturday at approximately 6 o'clock and, seemingly, had returned for his Austin Healey Sprite, registration number unknown to the landlord, probably sometime on Monday afternoon, though no-one had actually seen him. The landlord, a Mister Thomas Henshaw, was relating this to the police because it seemed odd to him. After Tom Henshaw had gone on his way, the sergeant, unaware of any significance of what he had just been told, read through his notes and offered to himself:

'Waste of time that was.'

Five minutes later, having passed on details to the backroom, he was soundly rebuked by his superior, with:

'Don't you ever read any of my emails, Sergeant Jameson!'

An hour later PC Craven arrived at The Inn, alone. David Tanner was spending the morning going through his notes, texts and emails from the past three months to see if there was information from Peter Wilson that would give a clue to what had happened over the last few days. There wasn't.

The uniformed officer sat in the empty bar with Tom Henshaw, going through Peter Wilson's visit. He'd arrived on Saturday morning, between 8.30 and 9.30, in the Sprite which he parked in the pub car park. He was booked in by Mrs Henshaw and left his luggage in his room, Room 2, before setting off on a walk. He returned late afternoon but told Mrs Henshaw that he had to leave and booked out between 5 and 6, for some reason leaving the Sprite behind. The car remained in the pub car park until Monday afternoon, when someone unseen took it, no doubt that someone being Mister Wilson.

Craven studied his notes.

'Can I have a word with your wife, sir?'

'Sally! The police officer would like a word with you.'

Sally Henshaw had, in fact, been listening intently from behind the half-open kitchen door. She came through and smiled nervously at Craven, sitting to the side, not close, in the unlit bar, with her hands clasped together. Craven stared at her, as did most men, but he didn't recognise her as the driver of the sportscar he'd seen on the Monday morning in Hawes. That view of her, with golden hair tossed to the wind, had been all too fleeting. He read to her his notes.

'So, Mrs Henshaw, is what your husband has told me, from your point of view, totally accurate and complete?'

'Yes, I think so, officer,' she replied in a very thoughtful manner.

Craven glanced from one to the other and then said:

'So, you are sure that the sportscar was here, in the pub car park, until mid-afternoon on Monday?'

The PC's voice made Tom Henshaw nervous. It had become very staccato. He glanced at his wife.

Sally Henshaw managed a smile, but her mind recognised the emphasis on 'until mid-afternoon'.

'Well, to be honest officer, mid-morning on Monday I got the bus down to Skipton to meet my husband for lunch. I left the pub by the front door and never actually looked in the car park to see if the sportscar was still there. When I

42

got back, mid-afternoon, it had gone. So, really, I don't know when Mister Wilson got it. But definitely before three thirty I'd say.'

Tom Henshaw was a little puzzled. The story seemed to be evolving, not fixed. However, Craven completed a note, nodding vigorously.

'Yes, that makes sense, Mrs Henshaw. You see, we believe the car was seen elsewhere on Monday morning. Thank you. You've been very helpful.'

'Do you know any more about Mister Wilson, officer?' asked Tom. 'I came down to Skipton this morning because my wife and I had got a bit worried about him.'

Craven tried to be matter-of-fact.

'Oh, no need to worry. He is officially missing but we're not overly concerned. Thank you for your time, both of you.'

He stood up and left, satisfied with what he had been told, but wondering what David Tanner would make of it all.

Sally Henshaw was much relieved. Hopefully, the police's attention would now be diverted elsewhere. Tom, however, was re-running the last few days and everything his wife had told him.

Mid-summer in Wharfedale was at its most idyllic on that Wednesday evening. It was still bright with hot sunshine and greenery everywhere. Sally Henshaw didn't appreciate any of this as she wound her way uphill from Cray in her own small red hatchback and turned right down the tarmac road to Scargill Cottage. She'd bought the cottage at the age of twenty-three, almost five years ago, along with a few acres and a couple of buildings in bad repair, from the farmer who owned Scargill Farm next door, and who, with a bad habit of backing slow horses, needed money quickly. She'd got a bargain, although that mattered little to her. In her first six months there, she'd had the cottage done up to suit, and extended. It came into view as she passed between two screens of conifers that Jonny had planted on his arrival. She parked her car against the small stone garden wall in front of the cottage, next to the familiar black SUV. She didn't bother knocking on the stout oak door before entering. She knew where Jonny would be, assuming he was there. She entered the living room, turned left through the stone-floored kitchen and tapped on the door to the extension. Jonny shouted:

'Come in, Sis.'

He had watched her arrive on screen via one of the many security cameras mounted outside. He was sitting at a huge desk arrayed with laptops, monitors and tablets, watching avidly as share prices went up and down in seemingly chaotic fashion around the world's stock markets. He turned and jumped out of his seat, placing both hands on

Sally's shoulders and planting a wet kiss on her bright red lips. He was clearly happy, excited and full of energy.

'I've made over a hundred thousand pounds today!' he bragged.

Sally shook her head in a knowing way, pleased that he was Jonny again.

'Brilliant, darling boy, but have you thought through Saturday? Tell me how the man got inside and how he ended up dead. Mother told me that you shot him with a pistol.'

'Oh, Sal! Must I? Everything is fine! He's up on Mastiles Lane now. Burnt to a crisp with no face.'

He sat back down, laughing as he rotated slowly on his computer desk chair.

'Jonny!' she shouted. 'I got rid of his car and I've had to make things up as I go along with Tom and, today, a young constable turned up. If Wilson was just a walker, we may get away with it, but if he wasn't, then others will follow him here.'

Jonny stopped rotating and his mood changed in an instant.

'Then I'll kill them too,' he said coldly.

'No Jonny. This must stop, now. Tell me about Saturday.'

He adopted the pose of a petulant teenager but did as he was told.

'On Saturday, around 10 o'clock, there was a man dressed in the usual walker's gear, whistling his way along the tarmac towards the cottage. He knocked on the door. Mother had watched him and opened the door. He said he was a bit lost and wanted to know how to get to Hubberholme. He walked straight in past her and continued chatting. Friendly! But then he started to ask mother questions, about how long she'd lived here and whether she was on her own. Mother didn't like that and so she came through to my room to get one of those small tourist maps. I went into the kitchen with the map, although you know that I don't like to be seen by outsiders. The man was standing in the middle of the kitchen floor with his phone. He looked at it, stared at me and then moved forward, smiling. It was then that I seemed to know, for certain. He knew me, Sally, he knew me. He reached inside his right-hand pocket and I could tell what he was going to do. So, I hit him, hard, very hard, like you know I can. There was a bang and he crumpled to the floor, hitting his head on the stone. He was dead!'

Yes, she knew very well how her brother could hurt someone. He was slight in stature and, to those that did not know, appeared weak and almost effeminate. This was far from the truth. Jonathan Maxim had been taught well by his father, and his father had been employed by the British Secret Service to kill on demand.

'Is that the whole truth?' she asked. 'You didn't shoot him?'

46

'No,' replied Jonny. 'Mother lied like mother does.'

'Where's the gun, Jonathan?' she asked sternly.

'I don't know,' he replied, sheepishly. 'But walkers don't carry guns.'

'You get some rest now. You need sleep. I'll get the supplies from the car and stock up the kitchen.'

She kissed him on the forehead and left the high-tech room, with its bed in one corner, and en suite facilities in the other. He started to undress, happy again.

Sally searched the rest of the cottage but found no gun.

After re-stocking the kitchen, she left the cottage and sat for ten minutes in the hatchback, engine running. Coldly, she felt better about the dead body on Mastiles Lane. No, walkers don't carry guns. The life of her brother meant infinitely more to her than the death of a probable MI5 officer. As for her father, four years earlier, when drunk one night, he had struck his beautiful daughter across the face, in front of his own son. He now lay buried in the woods nearby.

THURSDAY THE FIRST WEEK IN JULY

Thursday morning was drizzly and cool, with Skipton adopting a gritty Yorkshire pose. Craven was seated opposite Tanner, sipping on a hot coffee, retelling his visit to The Inn.

'It all makes sense, Wilson booking in, having some sort of walk and then booking out in a hurry. But why did he leave the car behind? And then there's the car itself. Did Wilson take it from the pub? We don't know for sure. We do know that the Sprite ended up in Hawes and that Peter Wilson had said he might go to the cheese factory according to Mrs Wilson. I'm certain I saw a woman in Hawes driving a Sprite on Monday morning and, more than likely, it was that very car.'

Craven sat back with his coffee waiting for a response. Tanner just frowned.

'There's something wrong, something we're missing. Let's suppose that Peter Wilson did as Mr and Mrs Henshaw claim. He leaves the pub without his car. That suggests that he was looking for something or someone nearby. He must have expected to return for the car. Maybe he spent the time observing a location or a person and then returned and took it. If he'd found anything, he would have contacted me, surely, but he didn't.'

At that moment Superintendent Blair's secretary shouted across to them. It was ten o'clock. They had been summoned.

Blair was leaning forwards with elbows on his desk, supporting his head with interlocked fingers under his chin. He sat back in his chair as the two men took their seats.

'Well, gentlemen,' he began, 'tell me what you've been up to regarding the Peter Wilson case.'

PC Craven respectfully went through events of the previous day. It was then Tanner's turn. He told Blair that he'd checked through all recent communications with Peter Wilson who hadn't seemed any closer to finding the man in question. He'd then consulted his bosses in London on the matter. Blair looked decidedly annoyed. His words were clipped.

'Thank you, PC Craven. As for you, Mr Tanner, a nice way of saying nowt. Yesterday, police officers questioned hoteliers, pub owners, shopkeepers and members of the public in Hawes and thereabouts, the last sighting of that blue sportscar. What did they come up with? Surprisingly, they found out that there is another similar Sprite, owned by a fifty-year-old lady who lives in Bainbridge, barely four miles from Hawes. They identified roughly ten people who had seen such a car in Hawes at the weekend, and seven people, when shown a photograph of Peter Wilson, thought they might have seen him in Hawes recently, including two ladies who work at the cheese factory. Make of that what you will.'

Craven shifted uneasily in his chair. Tanner smiled. Blair continued.

'I'm afraid I can't give any more resources to this currently. I even had a helicopter out all afternoon yesterday combing the hillsides around Hawes, to no avail! I would like to put out a missing person alert through local media this weekend. I've had a phone call from Mr Jack Wilson. The family are concerned at the lack of progress and are very upset. If Peter Wilson has gone missing because of what he was doing on your behalf, or MI5's, I need to know more. Who was he after, and why?'

'Yes, I see that, Superintendent. I can tell you a little more, but with confidentiality a must have.'

Blair nodded.

'We are searching for a man called Michael Maxim, about 55 years old, short, dark, military build. He was recruited by us after serving as an SAS officer in Iraq. Let us say that he was carrying out 'black ops' for us abroad.'

'You mean he was a killer on your behalf,' Blair said starkly. 'So, what went wrong?'

For the first time in the meeting, Tanner showed signs of nerves. He'd never had to deal with the likes of Blair before, a worldly-wise straightforward tough Yorkshire policeman.

'The truth is that, five or six years ago, Michael Maxim became a liability to MI5. He may have suffered PTSD after Iraq or maybe it was just the drink. He'd always had a bit of a drink problem. We paid him well enough, but he had a sideline in violence outside the law. It was very lucrative for him, but unacceptable to the Service. He began to employ his own son, Jonathan Maxim, to work alongside him. He'll be almost thirty now, an extremely bright boy, university educated, but completely beyond the edge of any spectrum. Together, they were a time bomb waiting to go off, and it did, resulting in the death of a Garda officer, two miles the wrong side of the Irish border. The decision was made to decommission them both, but it went wrong. Two of my colleagues lost their lives, and the Maxims disappeared.'

'Disappeared!' shouted Blair, 'I wish they had bloody disappeared. Are you telling me that two killers, one employed directly by MI5, are somewhere in Wharfedale? But how could two lunatics conceal themselves in a quiet community like this? Time bombs explode, no matter where they are.'

'That is our problem, sir. They must have someone supporting them in the dale. They're too volatile on their own.'

'Are there any family connections with the Dales, any other Maxims, or do you think that they have enough money to pay for their invisibility?' Blair remained angry but was thinking too.

'Michael Maxim was brought up in Lower Wensleydale, but both his parents are dead. He has a wife and daughter, but we haven't been able to trace them either. As for the money he has, we have no idea, but we suspect a lot.'

'So, there could be four Maxims floating around the dale. That's a lot of Maxims!' Blair was boiling over at this belated information.

'OK,' he continued, 'let's assume Wilson discovered something or someone between here and Hawes. We must find perhaps two people, or perhaps four, who settled in the dale in the past five years, hopefully visible but perhaps puzzling to the locals. I suggest that you and Craven check databases for incomers, boring as that may seem. There's a hell of a lot of second home owners in Wharfedale, but I can't spare manpower to help at this stage. We don't even know for sure that Peter Wilson is dead!'

'Oh, he is dead, sir,' Tanner added with certainty. 'As for going public through the media, that's OK by us, so long as it's just a simple missing person piece. The killer would expect that by now, anyway.'

'And finally, Mr Tanner,' said Blair, 'I don't suppose you happen to have a photograph of Michael Maxim or his son that we could use?'

'We do have an old army photograph of Michael Maxim, and one of his son Jonathan, at Cambridge, so both are around ten years out of date,' replied Tanner.

'Of limited use, I fear,' said Blair, 'but let me have copies anyway.'

The meeting ended with Blair emphasising that Tanner and Craven must make progress. Tanner felt uneasy, knowing that Blair would leak more information than desirable to the press if it suited him. He couldn't allow killers to remain on his patch. Better that they flee Wharfedale, rather than they kill again.

That afternoon, in the office provided by Blair for Tanner, Craven sat staring at a computer screen, scanning through umpteen databases he'd dredged up via the land registry, estate agents and electoral rolls, and any other government agency he could think of, giving details and partial details of incomers, holiday homes, rented and purchased properties, in Wharfedale over the past five years. Very quickly he recognised the uselessness of the task he had set himself. Eventually, he stopped and turned to Tanner who, seemingly, was dozing with a cup of coffee and the notes that Craven had taken over the past few days of the inquiry. Before Craven could utter a word Tanner telepathically opened his eyes and said:

'You'll get nowhere with that database stuff. We need to focus in on what we know. Peter Wilson, in my view, purposely went to Buckden, stayed at The Inn, and searched out a location or person nearby, and then disappeared. He may have got to Hawes, or not. Let's concentrate on incomers within walking distance of The Inn, three miles say. Villages, farms, holiday cottages. What does that give us?'

Craven swore under his breath, with a mumbled 'could have said that two hours ago.'

Tanner laughed out loud.

'Well,' continued Craven, 'you're talking about Starbotton, Buckden, Hubberholme, Cray, a chalet park, a caravan site, several farms and isolated houses, and a hell of a lot of sheep.'

'Forget the sheep,' said Tanner. 'Carry on constable. Back to the databases.'

Craven uttered an expletive as Tanner left the office.

An hour later, he suddenly became animated, nodding vigorously to himself while his feet bounced up and down excitedly. In that time frame, in that very small area of Wharfedale, one name, and only one name, had come up twice in his interrogation of the house sales database. That name was a Miss Sally Law.

At age twenty-three, approximately five years ago, she had purchased Scargill Cottage, Cray, for the sum of £138000. No mortgage was involved. It was apparently a cash purchase.

At age twenty-four, she had purchased The Inn, Buckden, for the sum of £212000. Again, no mortgage was involved.

Hardly able to contain himself, he checked the marriage registry. Yes, Miss Sally Law had indeed married Mister Thomas Henshaw just three years ago and currently resided at The Inn.

He then checked the electoral register regarding Scargill Cottage. No name came up.

At that moment Tanner came through the door.

'How many twenty somethings have three hundred and fifty thousand pounds in cash to splash out on a couple of properties here in Wharfedale?' asked Craven.

For the next half hour, Craven meticulously went through the details of what he'd discovered. Of course, there were lots of unsuspicious explanations, such as the bank of mam and dad, or a lottery win, or an inheritance, but it could be that Peter Wilson had stumbled on something, just as Craven had, and had targeted The Inn and Scargill Cottage. It was certainly worth investigating. They would try to find out more about Miss Sally Law and her family background. So, for Craven, it was back to that computer screen. Tanner decided that he would pay a visit to The Inn and that he might stay a night or two!

At midnight on Thursday, Tom Henshaw was lying in his bed, staring at the ceiling, watching a spider walking upside down in a random fashion from the window to the light fitting in the middle of the room. He was very tired and the last few days had disturbed him. Sally had been very much a mystery to him since the day they'd met, when she'd walked into his struggling pub and offered to buy the business and save him from going broke. He'd never really asked her much about life before Wharfedale. Frankly, he had been intoxicated by her and loved such intoxication. Inside, he knew that something was very wrong, her evolving story of the events over the last few days, her manipulation of him. He may not be a bright man, but he was no fool. Nevertheless, he would protect her with every breath in his body, of that he was certain.

There was a gentle knock on the bedroom door. Sally entered the room, wearing only a long pink diaphanous nightgown. Without speaking, she slipped into the bed beside him. They made love in total silence. She lay next to him, clinging gently to his chest, purring as she slept. Tom stared at the ceiling once more, joyous in his love for this blonde vision and her need for him. Soon, he fell into deep sleep and, when he awoke that Friday morning, he was alone again in his bed, but calm and happy.

FRIDAY THE FIRST WEEK IN JULY

It was ten thirty when Tanner alighted from the Dales bus in Buckden and walked across the road to the already welcoming door of The Inn. He entered, turning left into the lounge bar, empty except for Tom Henshaw who was wiping down tables ready for his day.

'Good morning,' smiled Tom breezily, 'you look like a walker, just off the bus, eh?'

'Yes,' replied Tanner, 'thought I'd book in for tonight if you do bed and breakfast. A local told me there were some good walks around here. I'm a southerner myself.'

'You don't say,' smiled Tom again. 'Yes, we do an excellent b and b and we have a couple of vacant rooms so, no problem. And there's loads of walks around here. Buckden Pike and the Triangle Walk are the most popular I'd say, five or six miles each. Probably a bit easy for regular walkers.'

'I'm only a fun walker, just up here for a weekend of fresh air, getting away from London. I'll take a room if I may.'

'Interested in the price?' asked Tom. 'It's fifty-five pounds for the night and full English.'

'That's fine,' replied Tanner.

Tom showed Tanner to Room 2, gave him the key and then left him to it. He'd eyed Tanner up and down as he'd entered the pub. He looked very clean, very tidy, and his walking shoes, shorts, polo shirt and backpack were obviously brand new.

'Maybe he's out of London, first time walking in God's county,' thought the landlord.

Thirty minutes later, Tanner sauntered into the bar where Tom was serving his first two customers of the day, two old men who often turned up to have a pie and a pint for lunch, along with a good natter about life in general.

After waiting his turn, he asked for a coke and ice, much to the other two's surprise.

'Which walk do you suggest for today, landlord?' asked Tanner.

'The name's Tom, Tom Henshaw, Mister Tanner. Well, the Triangle Walk is the obvious one I'd say.'

'I had a look in my walks book and it suggested either way round. Which way do you think?'

'Oh, I'd go to Hubberholme first, myself. Gentler start to the walk, and there's The George for an early stop if you fancy a snack before the climb,' replied Tom.

'You've got a great pub here, Tom. You must do well, with all the tourists and walkers. Been here forever, I suppose?'

'Yes, since I was a kid. My dad had it before me.'

At that moment, Sally Henshaw walked from behind the kitchen door into the bar and smiled at her husband. Momentarily, Tanner was stumped for something to say. Craven's description of her now seemed like a vast understatement.

'Katy needs you in the kitchen, dear,' she said. 'Some problem with the menu. Roasties.'

Tom muttered to himself and hurried through to the kitchen.

'You must be Mrs Henshaw?' said Tanner. 'My name's David Tanner. Here for b and b and a good walk or two.'

'Well, I hope you enjoy your stay, Mister Tanner. The Dales are beautiful this time of year.'

She turned her back on him and left the bar, hurrying upstairs to her bedroom. She grabbed her phone from the bedside table and, trembling, punched in Jonny's number.

'Hello, Sis, what's up?' said Jonny, playfully.

'I'll tell you what's up, brother!' she said sternly. 'A man called Tanner has turned up at the pub. He says he's here for a walk, staying tonight, but he's no walker, Jonny. He's one of the three men who came for you and father. He's MI5, I'm certain!'

'Hell! Yes, I remember Mr Tanner. He didn't recognise you?'

'No, Jonny, think. I was across the street from the safe house, in the car, waiting for you both. I got a good look at them, but they didn't see me. I saw them go in and then all hell broke loose. He was the one who got out alive. He was the one who ran away. He may be looking for the cottage, so you've got to stay out of sight.'

'He must be working with the man I killed. Do you think he knows about you, Sal?'

'I don't know. He might just be retracing Wilson's footsteps, so he's here at The Inn to search around. If he really knew where you were, or who I was, we'd have had it by now. I think this guy Tanner is playing percentages. After all, the body's nowhere near and hasn't been found yet, as far as we know, and Wilson's car was found over in Hawes. Just stay low.'

'What if he turns up at the cottage?'

'Mother can deal with him. He can't know about mother. But Jonny can't be seen.'

'OK, Sal. Let's keep our nerve, but if he gets too close, or figures out who you are, we'll have to get rid of him.'

'No Jonny, no more killing. If he gets too close, we'll have to disappear again, with the money and the toy! Think it out, gorgeous boy.'

'No problem,' replied Jonny, happy that his sister would use his brightness. 'Big kiss.'

With that, their conversation ended. Sally stood by her bedroom window, watching Tanner crossing the road and heading in the direction of Hubberholme. She composed herself and then went down to the bar where she poured herself a double whisky which she downed in one, observed by Tom, sitting in the corner of the bar with his two regulars. He got up and walked across to his wife.

'You OK, Sal?' he asked.

'Yes,' she replied. 'Just a headache. Had mother on the phone. She sounded a bit depressed, that's all. I may pop up to see her later, or maybe not. I might just help out that handsome husband of mine.'

It was only midday and the lunchtime rush still an hour away. Tom suggested that Sally lie down for a while. She returned to her bedroom window. In the distance she could see a lone walker consulting a map.

'Take care, Jonny my boy,' she whispered.

Tanner had the Triangle Walk route detailed on the OS map he carried, with each farmhouse, including Scargill Cottage, ringed in felt tip. His first stopping point was Hill Farm just above Hubberholme. Anyone doing the walk would go through Keith Clarkson's farmyard, part of the public footpath. The farmer was carrying a bucket of chicken feed to an old-fashioned hen house as Tanner approached with a wave of his hand.

'Excuse me, sir, Mister Clarkson I assume,' said Tanner, feeling inside a pocket to show his identity card. 'My name is David Tanner. I need to ask you a few questions regarding last Saturday.'

The farmer was taken aback by the immediacy of the statement, even more so when he carefully examined the identity card which seemed to indicate that the man before him worked for Special Branch. He remembered the previous Saturday very well. In the morning, a young man, clearly rather lost, had headed out of the farmyard the wrong way, obviously going to be in trouble when he got to the foot of the crag. The only other walkers he'd seen were a family and about a dozen oldies who'd come down off the terrace and down into Hubberholme on Saturday afternoon. Tanner showed him a photograph of Peter Wilson.

'No, sorry, never seen him up here,' said the farmer.

'Thank you for your time, Mister Clarkson. Please make no mention of my visit to anyone,' said Tanner with finality.

He strode off through the farmyard, soon heading left up an easy path to the top of the crag. There, he turned right along the flat terraced walk with Scargill Farm to his left. A few hundred yards away he could see a man carrying a shotgun over his shoulder. Tanner tapped his shoulder holster through force of habit. As he approached the man he relaxed.

'You must be Mister Denby, owner of Scargill Farm. Delighted to meet you sir. Can we have a chat about Scargill Cottage? My name's Tanner, I'm with Special Branch.'

Fred Denby, a typically overweight elderly Yorkshire farmer, looked dumbstruck, but didn't even ask to see any proof of identity.

'Better come in the house,' said the farmer. 'I'll pour us both a whisky. I need one if you don't! I could say what the hell's going on but you're probably going to tell me anyway.'

He broke the gun and turned away, plodding towards the farmhouse. Five minutes later he was sat opposite Tanner in the sparsely furnished living room, with his Racing Post set out on the table between them. He was a ruddy-faced widower who enjoyed his whisky and enjoyed the horses.

'This conversation is completely confidential,' stressed Tanner. 'First, have you ever seen this man, Peter Wilson, walking around up here? Maybe last Saturday?'

Farmer Denby shook his head at the photograph.

'You used to own Scargill Cottage, towards Cray, Mr Denby. Can you tell me who bought the cottage, were there any odd circumstances regarding the sale, and who's been living there for the past five years? Any information you can give me would be most helpful.'

'You ask a lot of questions, Mr Tanner, but no doubt you have good reason,' said Denby.

The farmer became very animated. He'd been very short of money at the time and had sold the cottage at a knock down price to a young lady, a Miss Sally Law, quite a looker, and her mother, Mrs Elaine Law. They'd paid in cash, probably the mother's money, he thought. They were both incomers, from down south. Soon after, they'd got a local builder to extend the cottage and install a lot of outside lighting and security cameras, not unusual for townies. Then, maybe a year or two later, the young one had moved out. She'd married Tom Henshaw, landlord of The Inn at Buckden.

'And, as far as you know, only the mother has been living there?' asked Tanner.

'Interesting question, young man,' said the farmer, having just finished his second large glass of malt.

'I don't know of anyone else living there. I've only seen the good-looker, Miss Law as was, coming and going, and her mother, Mrs Law, who has a big black SUV. I've heard someone shooting in the woods near to the cottage, at odd times, near dusk or very early in the morning. That's a bit queer but probably a local from Cray. You get a lot of walkers up here, half lost, and some idiots careering about on quadbikes where they shouldn't.'

'You've never visited the cottage since you sold it?' asked Tanner.

'No, young man, I keep to myself since the wife died. I didn't like how much they paid for the cottage though. Far too cheap. Still, finances are fine now.'

'How's that?' asked Tanner, suspecting the answer.

'I back faster horses, these days,' laughed the farmer.

Tanner joined in with the laughter and then shook hands with the now jovial farmer, who offered, 'Mum's the word, Mister Tanner. Mum's the word.'

Outside the farmhouse, Tanner studied his map carefully to decide on the best way to approach Scargill Cottage without being seen. He'd already decided not to walk up to the front door, knock and see who was there. The worst-case scenario was that he could end up dead. No, today he would observe. He walked across three of farmer Denby's fields and approached the cottage through a dense wood. About a hundred yards into the wood he stumbled over a roughly-made small wooden cross in the ground that had obviously been there for quite a time. 'A pet burial,' he thought to himself as he replaced it vertically in situ. He then came to the edge of the wood about fifty yards from

66

the side of the cottage. There were two farm buildings visible behind it. He took a pair of binoculars from his backpack and, staying hidden within the trees, observed the cottage windows. He saw no movement within, although some window blinds were closed. He then skirted around to the front of the cottage, but moving away from it, eventually hiding himself in conifers at the entrance to the driveway. Suddenly, the front door opened and a very smartly dressed old lady appeared, car key in one hand, large shopping bag in the other. She briskly walked down the garden path and got in the black SUV parked by the garden wall. She took off down the tarmac drive at speed, making Tanner move quickly to conceal himself as she flew past before turning left towards Cray.

'Fast driver for an oldie,' thought Tanner.

Tanner remained where he was for over an hour, his binoculars focussed on the cottage windows. He saw nothing, he heard nothing. He was sorely tempted to break and enter to find out more but, today, he was playing a hunch. He had no real reason to suspect Sally Henshaw or her mother of having anything to do with Peter Wilson's disappearance. He would bide his time. After all, Craven would be trying to find out more about them. He had completed his scouting mission for now and decided to return to The Inn.

When he got back to the pub, he searched Room 2 thoroughly, just in case Peter Wilson had left anything hidden. He found nothing. He rang Craven and asked him what he'd come up with regarding Miss Sally Law and her mother.

'In terms of anything fishy, nothing at all. I've checked all the obvious data, birth certificates, previous addresses, even bank details where I could, and everything looks squeaky clean. Usually you find omissions or glitches in data, but none here. They're either exactly what they appear to be, or someone is very good at covering tracks.'

'Fine,' said Tanner. 'I did the Triangle Walk and came up with little. No-one I spoke to had seen Peter Wilson last Saturday. I saw Mrs Law but didn't speak to her and there was no sign of anyone else at the cottage. I'll stay here overnight and then get back to Skipton. I still feel uneasy though. Blair should be arranging a TV slot for tomorrow's local news, then, who knows?'

Tanner showered and smartened himself up for an evening meal in the small restaurant. After a substantial three courses and half a bottle of red wine, he moved through to the busy bar, where Tom Henshaw and Sally were being kept very busy by several locals and a walking party of ex-teachers on a summer catch-up. He seated himself at the bar with the intention of making casual conversation with the landlord and his wife. Every now and then he managed to snatch a few words with Tom, whereas Sally smiled her way through the whole evening at the other end of the bar.

He learned no more than he already knew and, just after ten, went back upstairs to Room 2.

At the same time, Jonathan Maxim, shotgun in one hand down by his side, had just exited the wood next to Scargill Cottage and was moving swiftly across the fields to Scargill Farm. He knocked heavily on the farmhouse door which, after some time, was opened by farmer Denby, who was more than a little worse for drink. He blinked his eyes at the man with the shotgun and said:

'Ah, come in, Jon my boy. Shot any rabbits? Got a present for me, I hope.'

Maxim smiled and followed the farmer through to the stark living room, where he was offered a glass.

'Not for me thanks, Fred,' said Maxim. 'So, you had a visit this afternoon as I said you would, and you only told him what I told you to tell him?'

Fred Denby nodded and smiled.

'I mentioned quadbikes and people shooting up here, but that only your mother lived at the cottage. And I said she and that beautiful sister of yours had ripped me off when they bought the cottage off this poor hard-up farmer.'

He burst out laughing.

'Good, Fred,' said Maxim. 'Our arrangement over the past five years or so has been very beneficial to us both, I'm sure you agree. And, frankly, helping my mother and I keep out of the way, as you might say, means that you can happily back as many horses as you like, stake money assured.'

'Yes, Jon,' replied Denby. 'Your business is none of my business, young man, and, if you don't mind me saying, that mother of yours is an absolute lady. Nevertheless, I hope you've got an envelope with you.'

'Oh, yes, double the usual amount as a bonus, Fred. A thousand.'

'Very generous, very generous,' smiled Denby. 'Feel free to shoot one or two of my rabbits on the way home, unless you'd like a snifter with me.'

'No thanks, Fred. Must get back. That man who was sneaking around outside the cottage this afternoon, you never know, he may turn up again.'

'By the way, he showed me a photo of a bloke he was looking for, a man called Wilson, I think. I don't suppose you or your mother have come across him?'

'I haven't, and I don't suppose mother has,' said Maxim. 'Never heard of him, must be a walker gone missing.'

Fred Denby nodded without thought and showed Maxim to the door. The two shook hands and then Jonathan Maxim jogged away across the field, loaded shotgun in one hand.

SATURDAY SECOND WEEK IN JULY

'Right, you two. Better go to the loo before we set off. It's a long way to Malham Cove.'

Marion Summers clapped her hands. Her husband Ian went off to the gents with Robert, aged five, while she took Amy, now seven, to the 'little girls' room' as she put it. It was over ten minutes before the children were ready to start their walk. They had to stock up on crisps, chocolate and fizzy drinks, all to be carried by their father in his sizeable backpack. Marion, a primary school teacher, was the organizer of this event. She would carry the map of the walk and would point out places and things of interest, flowers, birds, butterflies, sheep and the like. She hurried out of the café at Kilnsey, enthusiastically, accompanied by her two nattering children, Ian following behind, diverted by thoughts of his working week as a Skipton solicitor.

'Look to the left, children,' said Marion, as if still at school, 'that is Kilnsey Crag, a huge piece of limestone rock. From this angle it almost looks like a huge head, Darth Vader perhaps, don't you think? There are usually rock climbers all over it. It's famous for its difficulty.'

'Who's Dart Vaber?' asked Robert, very loudly.

Amy, unlike Robert, having seen Star Wars on TV with her dad, burst out laughing. Her father joined in and was chastised by his wife.

Marion consulted her map and theatrically pointed left, directing her troops along a footpath which, a hundred yards or so later, brought them to a large iron gate marking the start of Mastiles Lane. Ian pulled back the huge gate and closed it after they'd carefully crossed the cattle grid spanning the gateway. A few minutes later they came to the top of a rise and stopped. Set out before them was a magnificent view of Mastiles Lane winding its way down into a dip in the land before climbing, what seemed to all but Marion, endlessly skyward over the moor.

'See the lane over the tops,' said Marion, proudly. 'That's where we're going. Only about six miles to Malham, ish.'

The other three looked at each other.

'I'm only five,' complained Robert.

'And I'm only thirty-six,' added his father.

'Come on, dad, race you to the top,' said Amy.

'I can't race that far!' he replied.

Marion promised them all sweets when they got to as far as they could see and set off at fast pace. After a quarter of a mile they went through a wooden gate onto the Lane proper, a narrow drovers' road with six-foot-high dry-stone walls on either side. It was a very hot Saturday morning and, when they met the steeply rising ground, both children began to tire. It took them over forty minutes to get to the top of the climb. Just over the rise the whole family parked itself against a wall for a well-earned break and nourishment. Marion gave Amy and Robert a packet of crisps each and a bottle of pop to share. She halved a bar of chocolate with Ian who looked slightly aggrieved at his share of the spoils.

Marion then referred to her book and read out a potted version of the two-thousand-year-old history of Mastiles Lane.

'That's very interesting, dear,' said Ian, smiling, with more than a hint of sarcasm. Amy laughed.

'Yes, it is!' said Marion, with a stern glance at her husband. 'Right, everyone, time to go!'

Amy was picking up some red plastic string she'd found in the middle of the track. She quickly shoved it in a pocket of her blue jeans. Robert had just gulped down the last of the pop.

'Need a wee first,' he shouted at his dad.

'Oh, Robbie,' said his mother. 'Lift him over the wall, Ian. He won't do it in front of his sister.'

Ian Summers climbed up onto the dry-stone wall, ready to lift his five-year-old. He glanced down and was met with a vision of horror and a fox staring up at him. The fox, showing no fear of human kind, had a bloodied red muzzle and was tearing flesh from an eyeless body, ravaged over the past week, not only by the fox but by rats, carrion crows and maggots. The man recoiled in terror, falling backwards off the wall, landing at Marion's feet. He leaped up and clung to his wife, panic stricken, whispering to her what he had just witnessed.

'Don't look, Marion, don't look. Get the kids back to Kilnsey. I'll stay here for the police,' he added, desperate for his children and his wife not to see the sight that would cling to his memory forever. He took out his mobile phone. The signal was weak, but he thanked God it was there. After making a call and trying desperately to stay calm, he looked back over the wall. The fox was nowhere to be seen.

That beautiful mid-summer Saturday morning, Superintendent Blair was walking slowly around his office, trying to compose for himself the words he would say to the press and TV at 2 o'clock regarding Peter Wilson, a resident of Skipton who had been missing for one week. At 11.53 his phone rang.

It was at three o'clock when Blair and Tanner arrived at the scene on Mastiles Lane in the police landrover driven by PC Craven. There were three other vehicles already there, and a police helicopter some hundred yards away, safe on flat ground. A large area around the body had been taped off, a small white marquee had been erected, and there were at least six uniformed officers plus a forensic team suited in white combing the area, while two forensic specialists were examining the body itself in detail. The chief forensic officer spotted Blair and approached.

'Good afternoon, Doctor Jones. What can you tell me so far?' asked Blair, coldly, with no emotion.

Jones was an expert pathologist, with over thirty years of experience.

'From the decay in the body tissue, and degradation via carrion, etcetera, I'd estimate that he's been up here approximately one week. He's been shot in the face. Shotgun pellets are everywhere, but he was dead when he was shot so he was probably killed or died elsewhere. Cause of death unknown, until he's examined back in the lab. Identity? Well, his face is blown away and an attempt has been made to burn the body but with very limited success. Certainly, there's no problem regarding DNA of course. We've pretty well finished up here now, so I suggest the body is removed to my lab back in Leeds. No doubt your boys will want to continue searching the area for some considerable time.'

Blair nodded. 'Thank you, Doctor. As much information as you can give me within 24 hours would be much appreciated. I know it's unusual, but I'm taking charge of this one myself.'

The two shook hands.

Within five minutes the body of Peter Wilson was on board the police helicopter.

Blair then spoke with Detective Inspector Tate, who was senior officer in charge of the crime scene, emphasising the need for absolute thoroughness and detail in his report which he required by the end of the day.

PC Craven drove Blair and Tanner back down Mastiles Lane to the café in Kilnsey where police officers were interviewing the Summers family with great care and empathy. The café had been closed to the public and a policewoman was sat at the far side of the room, doing a jigsaw with Amy and Robert, and making sure they had enough crisps and pop. A Detective Sergeant was interviewing Mr and Mrs Summers who were sipping on cups of coffee. Ian Summers had gone into shock and began to sob as his wife huddled close. As Blair entered the café, DS Trueman rose to his feet, looked across at his boss and shook his head. Blair nodded and left.

Back in the landrover, as the three of them headed back to Skipton, Blair said:

'Well, gentlemen, where does this leave us regarding any theories about how Peter Wilson met his demise?'

Tanner replied in a knowing manner.

'Peter Wilson was killed elsewhere. The killer blasted his face with a shotgun and set fire to his body. Unnecessary and pointless in today's DNA world. Those are the actions of someone who is severely deranged, the actions of Michael Maxim or his son or both. They're somewhere here in Wharfedale.'

Late that Saturday evening, Blair was sitting in his office, feet up on his desk, eyes closed, resting and thinking. His work day wouldn't be over for several hours yet. Four hours earlier, while going through the events of the last week in detail with DI Tate, he'd tuned into the local television news, knowing that, though theoretically he could have insisted on keeping the body on the moor out of the public domain, it would have been all over newsrooms by now, anyway.

It was the headline item.

'The body of a man has been discovered on Malham Moor, approximately ten miles from Skipton. The man is believed to be local and foul play is suspected. No further details are available at this time. Detective Inspector Alan Tate, of the Skipton police, will be making a statement to the press tomorrow morning.'

This short statement was followed, to the annoyance of Blair, by conjecture and misplaced rumour from a correspondent standing outside the café at Kilnsey.

There was a knock at Blair's door and DI Tate entered the room carrying a tablet, several sheets of paper, notepad and pen. He hurriedly sat down. Blair liked Tate. He was an extremely ambitious detective, twenty-seven years of age, and with such obvious ability that he would go places very fast.

'We may have had a bit of luck, sir,' he began, 'thanks to PC Warren, who was looking after the two children in Kilnsey café while my DS was interviewing Mr and Mrs Summers. The little girl, Amy, showed her a piece of plastic string that she picked up on Mastiles Lane near where the body was found. We believe that the body was tied up with it. We also found a fragment of stiff blue plastic trapped under the body, so it looks like the body was transported in a large plastic bag tied up with string, the sort of string that farmers use, baler twine. The lab boys are running DNA tests on the body tissue, the plastic and the string. They'll do comparisons with Jack Wilson's DNA, which was obtained this afternoon, and with the DNA profile of Michael Maxim that has been provided for us through David Tanner. Perhaps I shouldn't say this, sir, but I didn't find Tanner particularly helpful initially, even though I explained that I would be running the investigation on your behalf.'

'Yes, I know what you mean, Alan. I'm not sure I buy everything that I've been told by Mr Tanner. For the time being, let's leave young Craven working alongside him, but have a quiet word. He should report to you every morning. I do have friends in Special Branch, and I think I need to know more about Tanner and Peter Wilson. I'll give you contact details. Find out if Wilson was still MI5. As for the DNA, I got through to the lab earlier and leant on them a bit. They've promised me preliminary results by midnight. Doctor Jones should have completed the post-mortem by now and he's promised a heads up by midnight too.'

DI Tate smiled at Blair. 'Hell, you're good at your job,' he thought.

Blair offered Tate a coffee and a chocolate digestive. For the next forty-five minutes Tate went through all his paperwork with Blair and showed him photographs of the body and crime scene up on Mastiles Lane, and possible routes to and from the site that a killer could have used. He also sketched out his strategy for getting help from the local population. Had any locals seen anything unusual on the previous Saturday or Sunday, probably late at night? They also chatted about Wilson's car being found in Hawes on the Monday, possibly after his death it would seem, and the fact that Wilson had booked in at The Inn in Buckden on the Saturday morning, but had booked out without his car early the same evening. The two officers conjectured on the veracity of what they thought they knew. Someone had moved the car, but who? Perhaps Wilson, perhaps not.

At twelve o'clock, precisely, the phone rang.

'Yes, Blair here, what can you tell me about the DNA?'

Blair listened intently for some time, scribbling notes on his personal notepad.'

'Excellent, Kevin,' he said, 'I suggest you and your team get home and have a well-earned rest.'

He put down the phone and sat back in his chair, tired arms folded across his chest, and nodded at Tate.

'Those lab boys are brilliant, Alan,' he said. 'Body DNA matches with Jack Wilson's, so it is definitely Peter Wilson. And I think little Amy deserves a present from us all. There was no DNA found on the scrap of plastic but on the baler twine there were flakes of skin matching Peter Wilson's DNA and.'

He stopped as if teasing DI Tate.

'And,' he continued, 'traces of human sweat. No, the DNA isn't Michael Maxim's, but it is the DNA of a close male relative.'

'Jonathan Maxim,' said Tate with a smile and a clenched fist. 'So, Peter Wilson was killed or at least moved, by the son, but what about the father?'

There was a knock at the door and Doctor Jones, looking very weary, entered the office with 'I don't get paid overtime, you know, not like you police officers, just a small salary.'

Tate laughed at the bravery of the pathologist.

'Well, doctor, thanks for getting here so quickly. Now, tell me what you know,' said Blair.

Jones drew up another chair and collapsed into it, taking his report from his briefcase.

'The deceased had certainly sustained a nasty bump to the head. We found a slight fracture to the rear of the skull, probably caused by the head hitting a flat surface, but we don't believe that that is what killed him.'

At that, Jones stopped and stared annoyingly at Superintendent Blair, who smiled.

'Well what did kill him, since you obviously know, doctor?'

'We suspect that the bullet that we found lodged in his heart probably did the trick,' said Jones, displaying as so often in Blair's experience, his love of gallows humour.

'He was shot!' exclaimed Tate. 'But how come you didn't spot that up on the moor?'

'Easy to miss on a degraded body partly eaten and set fire to,' replied Jones with slight annoyance. 'The angle of entry, from between the seventh and eighth ribs on his right side, through the inside lining of his coat pocket, but not through the outside of his coat, is interesting, and from powder burns etcetera, suggests that the victim shot himself while his gun was in his pocket, possibly during a struggle. A small calibre automatic, it's all in my report. Rather lucky that that part of his clothing hadn't been burned but, well, a knotty problem for you.'

With that, he tossed his report onto Blair's desk, bade them both goodnight and went home to bed.

Blair stared at Tate in disbelief.

SUNDAY SECOND WEEK IN JULY

At ten o'clock on Sunday morning, on the steps in front of Skipton police station, DI Tate read a brief statement to the press. The body of a local resident, Peter Wilson, retired aged sixty-one, had been found on Malham Moor the previous day. He had been missing for one week and it was known that he had died elsewhere under suspicious circumstances and that his body had been moved by person or persons unknown to that location. Mister Wilson's last confirmed sighting was in Buckden on Saturday, eight days ago, although his car, a distinctive small blue sports car, was discovered in Hawes on the following Monday. Any person with information as to his whereabouts since that time should come forward to the police immediately. Photographs of Peter Wilson and of the car would be provided to the media forthwith. His immediate family have been informed and they request their privacy to be respected at this difficult time.

The Wilson household was grief stricken by the news that DS Trueman and PC Warren had brought them late on Saturday night. Jack Wilson hadn't realized how much he loved his brother and couldn't stop sobbing, something his wife had never seen. She'd always had a soft spot for Peter. He'd played more with Andrew over the years than his own father ever had. Andrew sat alone in his bedroom on that Sunday morning, upset but angry, angry that the police seemed to have done nothing over the past week. He'd tried to take in everything that the two police officers had told the family and there was one thing that was going round his brain constantly, the fact that Uncle Peter was definitely seen in Buckden on the Saturday, but that police could not confirm subsequent sightings of him in Hawes where he and his mother had discovered the Sprite. The police officers had refused to go into any more detail, much to Andrew's annoyance.

On Sunday afternoon Superintendent Blair chaired a meeting of a subset of his investigation team in the conference room at Skipton police station. Those present were Blair, DI Tate, DS Trueman, PC Warren, PC Craven, David Tanner and Blair's personal assistant who took notes in rapid shorthand, a rare skill these days. After a few opening remarks about the case, giving an overview, but lacking in detail, he asked PC Helen Warren to give her latest information. Not used to such a high-powered meeting, she started somewhat nervously but was encouraged by a smile from DS Trueman.

'Well, sir, yesterday, at Kilnsey, after the Summers family had left the cafe, DS Trueman and I did a house to house at the bottom of Mastiles Lane. I talked to Mrs Ann Dodd, a retired nurse who lives in a small cottage virtually on the junction with the main road. I asked her if she could recall anything unusual late at night the previous weekend. Apparently, sir, she sleeps very badly and often reads 'til two or three in the morning. She stated that, well after midnight on Saturday night, she was sure that she'd seen headlights coming down Mastiles Lane, lighting up her bedroom wall. She'd got out of bed and gone to her window, just in time to see a quadbike go past and turn left up the main road towards Kettlewell.'

PC Warren breathed a sigh of relief.

'Excellent, constable,' said Blair. 'What with your discovery of the baler twine and this new piece of information, you are to be congratulated. If you'd please wait outside, I'd like to see you again after the meeting. I may have another job for you.'

Helen Warren looked extremely pleased and confidently stood up and left the room.

DI Tate then gave a forty-five-minute presentation with the aid of his laptop and the screen at one end of the room, detailing the disappearance of Peter Wilson - last sighting, witness statements, crime scene evidence, DNA evidence, the pathologist's report, what he had learned from PC Craven and David Tanner, etcetera. He put his own perspective on the case and only failed to mention aspects that Blair had told him to keep to himself for the time being, primarily issues regarding MI5.

Blair then turned to Tanner who seemed shaken by the reality of the death of his long-time colleague and friend.

'Mister Tanner, I've been informed that you spent a night at The Inn in Buckden and actually did the Triangle Walk.

Apart from Sally Henshaw being able to buy Scargill Cottage, and then the pub itself, possibly with money from her mother, do you have any definite reason for suspecting the Henshaws in this matter?'

'No, sir, although The Inn was the last sighting of Peter Wilson and his car disappeared from there two days after he was probably already dead.'

'Good point, David,' said Blair. 'You didn't come across anyone who'd seen Peter Wilson on your walk, I understand, but you didn't interview Mrs Law at Scargill Cottage. Why not?'

Tanner shuffled in his chair, uncomfortable at the question.

'I observed the cottage very carefully to see if anyone else lived there, for an hour or so and then Mrs Law appeared and shot off in her SUV. I suppose that I'd started to doubt whether Wilson had been on the Triangle Walk. It was just a hunch that PC Craven and I had, coincidences mainly, about the Henshaws, tenuous I know. Wilson could have walked anywhere from Buckden. He could have checked out Starbotton or Cray, the local camp site or caravan park.'

'Indeed,' continued Blair 'but I agree that Wilson was looking for someone or was, at least, scouting around. I think you and Craven should interview Mrs Law to see if she saw Wilson. Let's eliminate your hunch. Go up there in a nice shiny police car. We now know that the Maxims are, or were, somewhere in the area. PC Craven has run the Laws through his databases, and everything checks out, but I'll see what I can find out another way. As for that blue sports car, I somehow think it holds the key. Who moved it and why? If not Wilson, why would the killer, unless there was something in it that he needed? Anyway, for now, let's end the meeting. DI Tate, DS Trueman, please stay behind.'

Tanner left the room with Craven and Blair's PA, feeling aggrieved at the way he had been dismissed by Blair. He needed to come up with something to get back in his good books. He'd got Michael Maxim's DNA profile sent up from London in no seconds flat, but felt that DI Tate, and even Blair himself, were suspicious of him, and suspicious of his motives. What's more, his own bosses in MI5 were unhappy and had queried what the hell he was up to, having never sanctioned the use of a retired MI5 operative in his search for Michael Maxim. Maxim may have been instrumental in the deaths of two MI5 officers, but he also knew far too much about MI5 covert operations within the UK, operations that were unknown to government, and operations that must never see the light of day. The fact that Maxim was lying low had suited his bosses. Their plan had been that when he eventually crawled out of the woodwork, he, and his volatile son, would have been dealt with. With the death of Peter Wilson, MI5 had lost control of events, and Tanner was feeling uncomfortably like a potential scapegoat.

As Tanner left the conference room, PC Warren went back in. Blair motioned her to sit down and then nodded to DI Tate.

'Helen, we'd like you to have a train ride to Suffolk for us. DS Trueman will give you details. This may come to nothing, but you seem to have luck on your side.'

Blair and Trueman smiled. PC Warren looked confused. Although they were smiling at her expense, she knew that as a lowly police constable she was being given an important task to fulfil in a high-profile murder investigation.

MONDAY SECOND WEEK IN JULY

When Craven had dug as deep as he could into the backgrounds of Sally Law, now Henshaw, and her mother, Mrs Elaine Law, he had come up with nothing suspicious, but the data had seemed too clean to him. He and Tanner had been surprised at Sally's ability to buy two homes in Wharfedale at such a young age, but there could be many explanations. The sale of even a modest home in London could easily finance two homes in Wharfedale. However, the Law's arrival in the area being five years ago, coupled with Peter Wilson staying at The Inn and apparently searching for someone locally, followed by his untimely death, meant that further checks must be carried out. Superintendent Blair needed to eliminate the Laws from the investigation, although in truth he had already reached the conclusion that Sally Law was very much a red herring and that, to mix metaphors, the birds had already flown. His view was that Peter Wilson had found Michael and Jonathan Maxim, that he had lost his life, and that the Maxims, one week on, would be far away. Nevertheless, early that Monday morning, Helen Warren, dressed smartly out of uniform, attended a short meeting with Blair. He explained what he wanted her to do. She was to make her way by train to a small town in Suffolk, Market Tatton, roughly halfway between Norwich and Lowestoft. According to Craven's data, Elaine Brooke had married James Law there, at Saint Peter's church, over thirty years ago. Elaine Law's only known address subsequent to that in Market Tatton, apart from Scargill Cottage, was in London some twenty years after that, where she was identified as widowed. Digitally, everything checked out. PC Warren's task in Market Tatton was to find physical evidence that confirmed the identity of Elaine Law and her daughter. At midday Helen Warren boarded the Leeds train to Peterborough, the first leg of her rather tortuous journey into rural Suffolk.

Shortly after, DI Tate knocked and entered Blair's office.

'I've just had a long conversation with your colleague, Mr Trevellyan in Special Branch, sir. He's found out some interesting information regarding Tanner and Maxim.'

'Excellent, Inspector,' replied Blair, impatient to know more.

Trevellyan, now a high-up in Special Branch, was a friend of Blair's back in the days when they both trod the beat as humble police constables. Formerly with the Met, he had several contacts within the Secret Service. He had learned that Tanner had been fast-tracked by MI5 and was so highly regarded that he had been seconded to work alongside the SAS in Iraq for MI6. It was there that he had met Michael Maxim, who had carried out operations on MI6's behalf. His career had taken a knock with rumours that he and Maxim had benefitted financially from artefacts looted from a Baghdad museum. This had gone down particularly badly with our American allies. Both men were recalled to the UK where Tanner was exonerated. He took up his MI5 duties again and Maxim was used, from time to time, in covert assignments within the UK, including dubious work in Northern Ireland. Maxim became unreliable and for some reason Tanner was posted north to Catterick Garrison, with a diminished role involving liaison with the Army. The fact that he had been searching for Maxim subsequently, and had used Peter Wilson to assist him, had, according to Trevellyan, not been part of his brief and was a matter of concern.

'So, what do you make of Tanner, now, sir?' asked Tate.

'I don't know,' replied Blair.

David Tanner glanced at his watch. It was 1.15 p.m. He tapped his shoulder holster before getting into the police car alongside PC Craven. Both men were extremely apprehensive. 'Nothing to worry about,' muttered Craven to himself as they left Skipton behind them, 'just a chat with an old lady.'

'You'd better be right,' added Tanner, embarrassing his colleague. 'We'll chat to Mrs Law and then try Cray and the campsite and caravan park near Starbotton.'

Tanner understood Blair's safety logic. If there was a dangerous Maxim up there at Scargill Cottage, turning up in a 'nice shiny police car' would immediately alert them to keeping their heads down. That thought gave no comfort to Tanner. However, he knew that he should have interviewed Mrs Law to confirm whether she'd seen Peter Wilson on that fateful Saturday. He would put that right. The two men continued their journey in silence and eventually drove up the road above Cray and turned right towards Scargill Cottage. The police car slowed to an almost halt as it proceeded between the conifer screens some two hundred yards from the house. They parked next to the black SUV and got out of the car. They stood a while, examining the windows, but saw no-one, taking in the many security cameras that seemed to be focussed on them.

'Looks shut up to me, as if no-one's in,' offered Craven.

The front door of the cottage opened and a petite lady, with heavy make-up and purple rinsed hair, dressed very smartly in a light blue summer dress, appeared before them.

'Hello officer,' she said very politely to the uniformed PC, 'we don't often see a police car up here. In fact, I've never seen a police car up here before. Is there something wrong?'

Craven and Tanner started to relax.

'No, Mrs Law. I assume you are Mrs Law?' said Craven. She nodded. 'I'm PC Craven and this is Mr Tanner. We don't wish to upset you, but you may have seen on the television that the body of a man, Peter Wilson, has been found up on Malham Moor?' She nodded again. 'We believe he was walking in this area last Saturday, that is, nine days ago, and we're asking people if they saw him. Just part of our enquiries.'

Craven handed her a photograph of Peter Wilson. The old lady studied it very carefully while Tanner shuffled from side to side, his eyes fixed on her and then on the windows of the cottage.

'Oh, yes, I've seen him before. It could have been on that Saturday, or the Sunday maybe.'

Craven and Tanner glanced at each other.

'Please be sure, Mrs Law, if you can. You saw him up here?'

'Yes, young man,' she continued. 'Definitely, that weekend. He was a walker and I think he'd got rather lost because he turned up at my door, and nobody does, usually, and he asked me the way to Hubberholme. I told him he needed to go right along the path just beyond the conifers. He seemed happy at that and off he went. The strange thing though is that he turned left, not right, and probably walked back down to Cray. It was definitely him.'

She handed the photo back to Craven and appeared slightly unstable on her feet.

'You should ask my daughter,' she continued. 'She runs the pub in Buckden with my son-in-law. They take care of me you know, keep me stocked up and everything. I don't get about much these days, what with my arthritis.'

'Thank you, Mrs Law,' interrupted Tanner, 'you've been very helpful. We must get on. Again, many thanks.'

Craven added his own thank you and the pair turned away and got back into the police car. As they drove off, Mrs Law waved them goodbye.

'What did you think of the old dear?' he asked.

'Very convincing,' replied Tanner, thoughtfully.

'Well, it seems to make sense,' said Craven. 'Peter Wilson walked up here, then returned to Buckden via Cray. At least we've actually found someone who saw him on the day he disappeared.'

'Yes, but why did he go back?' replied Tanner quizzically, his mind telling him that he'd missed something important in Craven's conversation with Mrs Law. He would replay it to himself later.

They drove down into Cray and knocked on a few doors. No-one recognised the photograph of Peter Wilson.

Late on Monday evening, Jonathan Maxim phoned his sister to tell her about the police car turning up at the cottage that afternoon.

'Mother did very well, Sal. She told the young police officer that she'd seen Wilson on the Saturday and that he'd headed back down to Cray. He seemed happy with that.'

'What about Tanner?' she asked.

'He didn't say much, but he watched mother and the cottage like a hawk. I couldn't tell what he was thinking, but he is a dangerous man, an intelligent man, and he'll be back. He will piece it all together, Sal.'

'Yes, he will, my gorgeous boy. It is time for us to get out. Move the money, Jonny. Dougie, as we agreed. Then, I want you to plan a route out by ferry, to Amsterdam. Do it all online. Use the name Brooke, but don't hide it. Leave it on the laptop.'

'I don't understand, Sal.'

'Don't worry,' she reiterated, 'I've thought it all out, except for Tom. I don't know what to do about Tom.'

She sounded upset and fell silent.

'Oh, Sis, don't cry. We'll take care of Tom.'

Jonathan Maxim kissed his phone and the call ended.

Back in his Skipton hotel room, David Tanner sat with a gin and tonic, thinking about Mrs Law and Sally Henshaw. On the face of it, he had no evidence against them. They appeared to be who they said they were, yet, underneath it all, he knew the truth. Too many things bothered him, but they were individually trivial. When Craven had interviewed Mrs Law she had said 'we don't get many police cars up here', we not I. She had recognised Wilson's photograph immediately, as if expecting to be shown it. He'd seen that in her eyes, and she'd seemed intentionally unsteady on her feet, even though, the day before, she'd moved swiftly to her SUV before roaring off like a boy racer. Yes, like a boy racer. What's more, although Tanner had observed no movement within the cottage, one of the security cameras had seemed to re-adjust its focus as he had shuffled from side to side, as if zooming in on him. He no longer believed that only one person lived up there at Scargill Cottage. However, none of this proved anything.

Tanner went into the bathroom to dowse his face with cold water to clear his head. When he came back into the room there was a man sitting in his chair, a very unhappy-looking large man, mid-forties, in an immaculate blue suit. The shock of seeing his boss, who Tanner had never seen outside his London office, rendered him speechless.

'Well, David, what a pretty mess you've got the Service into,' said Dawson, with unblinking eyes.

97

'Yes, sir,' replied Tanner, waiting for the hit.

'You see, after Maxim's misdemeanours in Iraq I gave you the benefit of the doubt, even though you were running his SAS team, not the other way around. And then there was the rather unfortunate incident across the water with the Garda officer. Not your fault I know, but I gave you the chance to make amends, anyway. But what happened at the safe house? Two men dead, David! And then, poof, the Maxims disappeared! Eliminating Michael Maxim was your last chance with MI5. Not only is he a killer, but with what he knows that man could put us all in jail, or at the very least, lose me my lucrative pension. I even gave you some more time to find Maxim and you failed.'

'Yes, sir,' said Tanner, his cooled forehead now beginning to sweat, 'but I think I've found him now.'

'Really, David. And no doubt the police think they've found him too, and the whole bloody world will know! Tell me, how have we got to this situation? How has Peter Wilson ended up dead, a retired officer who had never fired a gun in anger, an officer who had sat behind his desk for over twenty-five years. I sent you to Catterick Garrison, to Army liaison! It was a demotion, you were out of the game!'

'Yes, sir,' repeated Tanner, 'but Catterick was useful. Three years had gone by and we'd got nowhere back in London trying to find Maxim. He was brought up in the Dales and stationed in Catterick. It was a good call, but it took me time. Eventually, I became a drinking buddy with some ex-SAS guys who'd worked with Maxim. You couldn't get a word out of them, but one of them, after a lot of drink, became too trusting. He'd met Michael and Jonathan Maxim at a secret re-union, at some pub in Wensleydale, just over four years ago. He told me that Maxim was holed up 'in the hills' as he put it, either Wensleydale or Wharfedale.'

'And why the hell didn't you tell me or ask for help, instead of involving Peter Wilson?' exclaimed Dawson.

'You'd got rid of me, sir! I needed to sort this myself!'

'And can you sort this yourself, David, without police involvement, without the whole world crashing in on us? Michael Maxim can never end up in a court of law.'

'Yes, sir, I think I can, but should I?'

Dawson stared stoney-faced at David Tanner, knowing what he was asking.

'A successful end to this affair could mean a move back to London,' came the reply.

Tanner nodded. Dawson got out of the chair and left without another word.

In his bed that night, Andrew Wilson was thinking about what the two policemen had told the family after the body had been found. The last confirmed sighting of his uncle had been on the Saturday afternoon in Buckden. But why Buckden? He and his mother found the Sprite in Hawes on the Monday, yet police seemed unsure as to whether Uncle Peter had even got to Hawes. That didn't make sense. He decided he would go to Skipton police station the next day and find PC Craven.

TUESDAY SECOND WEEK IN JULY

PC Helen Warren, out of uniform for the first time as a serving police officer, left the Broads Hotel in Market Tatton at nine o'clock on that bright summer Tuesday morning in Suffolk, the task in hand firmly fixed in her head. This was the first time in her twenty-three years that she'd been outside Yorkshire, except for two holiday breaks, one with her parents to Florida when she was eight, and one with 'the girls' to Ibiza, a very drunken affair that previous summer.

Her first port of call today was St. Peter's church where she was in luck, immediately bumping into a young vicar who was tidying pews for some unknown reason. In the vestry, he quickly found marriage registers going back decades and confirmed that Elaine Brook had married James Law thirty-two years ago. He himself knew nothing of this but was able to point Helen towards the previous vicar, now well and truly retired, who lived in Marsh Lane, a Reverend Spink. Within twenty minutes Helen Warren was seated opposite the good Reverend, supplied with a small sherry, listening to his recollections from years gone by, trying to look interested. After fifteen minutes of inconsequential chat she became excited when he said:

'Of course, one thing I always did with my weddings was to insist on a wedding photo with the bride and groom. I've collected them over the years, you know. It's rather

101

nice to look back on these things don't you think? It gives one a feeling of self-worth, of contributing to the life of Market Tatton, and yes, I will have a photo of Mr and Mrs Law properly filed away.'

He crossed the living room to a very large Victorian bureau. Helen followed. He opened the third drawer down on the left to reveal what appeared to be a perfect card index system. He ruffled through the cards, going back in time from when he had retired, stopping at the appropriate year. He removed a small photo album which must have contained roughly twenty photographs, each with date and relevant names on the back.

'I know it's over thirty years, but here are Mr and Mrs Law for you. Elaine Brooke made a lovely bride don't you think?'

PC Warren took a photograph of the photo with her mobile phone and thanked the good Reverend effusively for his help. It would be up to DS Trueman and his bosses to decide if the photo was useful or not but what a great start to her day! She had been given a copy of the photograph of Michael Maxim, aged around forty to forty-five in army uniform and showed it to Reverend Spink who just shook his head and said:

'Too long ago, my dear. It could be the same man, or not don't you think?'

She agreed. She thanked him for his help and went on her way. Surprisingly, he never asked her why she had come all this way to ask about Mr and Mrs Law.

Her next stop was Lowestoft Road School, the local primary. Sally Law was born in Market Tatton and would have attended the school. As might be expected, Helen Warren was out of luck this time. The school had no records going back that far. However, she was pleased with her progress and headed for the nearest coffee shop. There, she had lunch and emailed the photograph with details to DS Trueman. She got an immediate response of 'well done, will check out.'

That afternoon Helen Warren spent her time at the local council offices, with harassed staff who were far too busy with their own duties to help with hers, attempting to find any data on the Laws during the years before they were known to have moved to London. Again, data was sparse, but she did obtain a family address at 11, Crook Avenue. It wasn't until late afternoon that she knocked on the door of the semi-detached house in a very quiet area of Market Tatton. No-one answered so she tried next door. A very old lady came to the door. She was most shocked to have a police identification card thrust at her, even though Helen smiled and explained why she was there in a relaxed manner. The lady seemed confused by the questions she was asked until the wedding photo was shown to her.

'Ah, yes, I remember, Elaine and Jim, ever so nice, at least she was, and they had a lovely little girl, can't remember her name though.'

'Sally?' offered Helen.

'Yes, Sally, that's it. She was a beautiful girl with yellow hair like golden corn.'

'Do you remember Mr Law, what he did?' Helen asked.

'Sorry, no, but Elaine was on her own a lot of the time. He could have been in the forces or worked abroad but, to be honest, I forget. I didn't really see much of him, but she was very nice.'

Helen's chat with the old lady stalled but she walked back to the hotel feeling very positive that everything seemed to check out with the Laws. Back in her room she made copious notes on her day and the information gained, and then emailed a short report to DS Trueman, copied to DI Tate. She received no reply. After having what she regarded as a superior three course dinner with wine, all on expenses, she spent the rest of the evening in front of her television screen, paying it no attention, wondering whether to return to Skipton in the morning. Or was there more she could do here in Market Tatton?

At around lunchtime, when DS Trueman had received the emailed photograph, he had immediately shown it to DI

Tate. They stared at the photo, comparing it to that of an older Michael Maxim.

'Could be, maybe not,' they both agreed.

'Give both photos to forensics,' said Tate. 'They're good at this sort of thing. Facial ratios and all that. You never know.'

It had been over a week since Andrew Wilson and his mother had discovered Uncle Peter's Sprite over in Hawes. It had seemed obvious. Peter Wilson had gone to Hawes, to the cheese factory, and had disappeared! The revelation that Uncle Peter had had a secret life, followed by the horrific news that his body had been discovered up on Mastiles Lane, well, the family was finding it hard to come to terms with. Andrew had become angry but also confused. If his uncle had gone to Hawes, how come his last confirmed sighting was Buckden? That suggested that he might have done the Triangle Walk, as he'd hinted at to his mother, on the same day as he himself had done the walk from Hubberholme. And that was the day he had been spooked by a gunshot near a remote cottage above Cray! He needed things cleared up by the police. Surely someone had seen his uncle in Hawes?

After brooding about it all morning, and without telling his mother or father, Andrew cycled to Skipton police station. Standing in front of the desk sergeant he demanded:

'I want to see constable Craven. It's very important. I'm the nephew of Peter Wilson.'

Sergeant Jameson looked him up and down, was about to say something he shouldn't, and then thought better of it.

'I'm afraid he is out on duty, sir,' said the sergeant. 'You could see Mr Tanner. They share an office together.'

Andrew was reluctant to see Tanner. From the night he'd turned up, everything had seemed to go wrong. Nevertheless, he needed information. He nodded at the sergeant and was pointed towards the left corridor, Room 5. After knocking and hearing a gruff 'come in' he entered the office to see David Tanner looking up at him from his desk, clearly surprised to see the young student again.

'What can I do for you, Mr Wilson?' asked Tanner, formally.

'It's about Uncle Peter. I was going to ask PC Craven. You see, I don't understand why the police have said that he was last seen in Buckden on the Saturday. How come? Mum and I found his car in Hawes on Monday. Surely, he was seen in Hawes? And when the two officers came to tell us he'd been found, it was up on Malham Moor, miles away from Hawes, or Buckden even, and that doesn't make sense.'

Andrew Wilson was getting very upset and was almost in tears. Tanner spoke quietly.

'I agree, Andrew. It is very puzzling. We do have more information than you know. Your uncle booked in at the pub in Buckden on the Saturday, probably had a walk, but then left late that afternoon without his car. You found his car on the Monday in Hawes. We've talked to many people in Hawes. Some say they might have seen him but there is no confirmed sighting of your uncle. That's why we said what we said.'

Andrew looked even more confused.

'Left Buckden without his car? That's daft.'

'Yes, it appears so,' continued Tanner, 'but he may have returned for it on the Monday morning and then driven to Hawes. We're not sure. The landlord didn't see who took the car, nor his wife.'

'So, he might have gone to Hawes like I thought, but you don't really know.'

'That's right,' said Tanner.

'And the landlady never saw Uncle Peter in Hawes?'

'What do you mean?' asked a stunned Tanner.

'Well,' said Andrew, 'I saw her in Hawes on Monday morning. Uncle Peter could have given her a lift there.'

Tanner's brain raced but his face and voice stayed as they were.

'Are you sure it was Mrs Henshaw you saw in Hawes?' he asked.

'Of course, although I don't know her name. She was standing at a bus stop. Absolute stunner!'

'Yes, she is,' agreed Tanner, smiling. 'So you see Andrew, we don't really know if your uncle got to Hawes, but he may have done. Interesting about Mrs Henshaw. It might not have been her, of course. Maybe another stunner over in Wensleydale,' he joked.

'I doubt that!' said Andrew Wilson, re-assured by what David Tanner had told him.

Tanner stood up.

'Thank you for coming in, Andrew,' he said. 'I hope I've helped. I can't tell you everything going on with the investigation, but, and it's a big but, I believe that we are very close to finding out exactly what happened to your uncle, and who killed him. Have confidence in us. We will get our man soon.'

Andrew wiped tears from his eyes and thanked Tanner. As he left Skipton police station and got on his bike, he saw PC Craven arrive back in his car. He nodded at him as he set off back home.

As he sat back down at his desk, David Tanner thought about what he now knew for certain. Sally Henshaw had lied to the police. On that Monday morning she had not got the bus from Buckden to Skipton to meet her husband. She had gone to Hawes, most likely, thought Tanner, in Peter Wilson's car, with or without Wilson. She had made it to Skipton around lunchtime, no doubt by taxi or by bus. If Peter Wilson had been killed before that Monday, as Dr Jones had thought more than likely, then Sally Henshaw was directly involved in the murder of Peter Wilson, or, at least, in a cover up of his murder. With everything else that he had put together, Tanner was now convinced that Sally Henshaw was the daughter of Michael Maxim.

As he managed a smile to himself, Craven came through the door.

'Has Andrew Wilson been in to see you?' asked Craven. 'I've just seen him leaving.'

'Yes, he just wanted some reassurance about the case.'

Tanner said no more and returned to the paperwork on his desk.

WEDNESDAY SECOND WEEK IN JULY

'Another sunny day in Suffolk,' thought PC Warren as she finished her breakfast before going through to the hotel lounge to sit with a coffee, waiting for DS Trueman to call. She'd received an email from him at 8 a.m. saying that forensics were analysing the two photographs. She was feeling a bit down. Trueman had asked for the name of the old lady she'd spoken to, asked if the old lady had said whether the Laws had a son as well as a daughter, and asked whether the name Maxim was known to anyone she'd spoken to in Market Tatton. She realized that she had a lot to learn.

Her phone rang at 9.35. She listened intently. Forensics had scrutinised the two photographs. Neither was of sufficient quality to say conclusively whether the groom and soldier were the same man, bearing in mind their difference in ages. It was described as a 50-50 call. Helen apologized to her boss for not being as thorough as she should have been yesterday.

'Not to worry, Helen,' Trueman said to raise her spirits, 'we think we've sent you chasing red herrings anyway, but it's good experience. Go see the old lady again and maybe the council. I'll be amazed though if any Maxims have lived in the town.'

She cheered up and walked quickly from the hotel to the council offices, to be met by 'oh no, she's back' looks from staff. After an hour or so, based on council tax receipts, electoral rolls and anything else that staff could come up with, Helen had established to her own satisfaction that no Maxim had ever seen the light of day in Market Tatton. She left the council offices, much to the relief of hard-working underpaid staff, and walked out of the town centre to Crook Avenue. Just in case, she knocked at number eleven, but again got no reply. 'They obviously work for a living,' she thought. As on the previous day, she then tried next door.

'Oh, it's you again,' said the old lady, rather brusquely. 'I'm going to the shops.'

'So sorry to disturb you again, Mrs?' PC Warren asked.

'Mrs Dean,' came the reply.

'Just another couple of questions, then I'll disappear,' she continued, smiling. 'Mr and Mrs Law, did they have any other children apart from the pretty golden-haired daughter?'

Mrs Dean thought very hard as if the last thirty years had taken a heavy toll on her memory. Finally, she said:

'I don't remember any other children next door. No, Elaine only had one child, I'm sure.'

'So, there was no son?' PC Warren said, irritating the old lady.

'No son, just the one daughter,' retorted Mrs Dean with equal emphasis. 'I only ever saw one child, except when Sally's cousin came to stay once or twice. Like two peas in a pod they were. Her name was Sally too, come to think of it.'

Helen Warren's mouth dropped open. She prompted the old lady to repeat what she'd just said as she noted it down, before asking:

'What was the other little girl's surname, Mrs Dean?'

The old lady took her time.

'No idea, dear,' she said, 'in fact, I'm not sure she was a real cousin, if you know what I mean. I think it was more that her mother was a good friend of Elaine's. They were both aunties, you know.'

'Do you know where the other little girl lived, Mrs Dean? Not here in Market Tatton?'

'Oh, that's a hard one, let me think. Well, what I do remember is that the girl lived with her mother and grandfather. I think he ran a pub, more towards Lowestoft. He'll be long gone by now I should think.'

For several minutes, Helen Warren tried desperately to help Mrs Dean remember more, but with no success and, when asked if the name Maxim meant anything to her, the old lady just shook her head.

She walked slowly back to the Broads Hotel, trying to assess whether she'd learned anything of use, or not. Should she consult her boss, or give up? But two, not one, golden-haired Sallys! She texted Trueman with 'Staying til tomorrow. Laws had no son. No Maxim in Tatton. Sally Law had friend named Sally. Investigating.'

When Trueman read the text message he was with DI Tate in his office. He read it out loud to the inspector and both burst out laughing.

'Hell, that girl's a trier,' said Tate.

Helen Warren ate an insubstantial lunch in a quiet coffee shop in the centre of Market Tatton, making notes as she consulted a local map on the tablet that she carried everywhere with her. She identified seventeen pubs between the town and the outskirts of Lowestoft. She tried very hard to ascertain the names of landlords and phone numbers and spent the rest of the afternoon drinking coffee and phoning round. She had many unfruitful conversations with pub staff but, by 5.30, when the coffee shop manager insisted on closing and throwing her out, she had eliminated eleven of the seventeen pubs, unable to make any progress at all with any of the other six.

'Give up for the day,' she said to herself as she walked back to the hotel. 'Well, they said not to worry about expenses. I'll hire a car for the morning!'

Back in the hotel, the receptionist was more than happy to hire a car on PC Warren's behalf.

'Would a BMW 3 Series be sufficient?' she asked.

'Oh, that would be perfect,' replied Helen, having no idea on cost for the day.

'It'll be outside the hotel for you at 9 a.m. tomorrow morning.'

'Excellent,' said the police constable, smiling. 'I think I'll have one of your marvellous three course dinners again tonight.'

At ten o'clock on that Wednesday morning, Superintendent Blair had held a meeting in his office with DI Tate and DS Trueman.

'Let me sum up. I think that Peter Wilson was killed by Michael Maxim and disposed of by his son, Jonathan Maxim. The likelihood is that the birds have flown and that it will have to be someone else who catches them, probably MI5, Tanner and his ilk. We'll continue to put limited resources to the case unless, for instance, we can prove any links to anybody else here in Wharfedale, such as Mrs Law and Mrs Henshaw. I doubt there is any link, even though that police constable of yours is doing her best in darkest Suffolk to prove there is one.'

Trueman and Tate smiled.

'Agreed, sir,' said Tate, 'but after what we've found out, I am concerned about Tanner, whether he's always on the right side of the law.'

'Yes,' said Blair, 'but that's more MI5's problem than ours. Just make sure you keep an eye on what he gets up to. Tanner will soon disappear, like all these secretives do, eventually. Now, let's move on. What's happening?'

Trueman and Tate ran through the rather prosaic details of the investigation in Wharfedale. Little more had been discovered. Several people remembered seeing a lunatic on a quadbike between Kilnsey and Kettlewell late on the Saturday night, but there are hundreds of quadbikes in the area. A couple in Cray had seen Peter Wilson walk uphill through the village on the Saturday morning, confirming to an extent what Mrs Law had said, although they had not seen him return. More people in Hawes remembered seeing a blue sportscar on the following Monday and, that morning a resident of Bainbridge had seen a Sprite heading out of the village towards Hawes, driven by 'definitely a woman', although police already knew that a lady in the village owned such a car. Finally, Tate informed Blair that a thirty-eight-year-old resident of Grassington, well known to police as not being of sound mind, had confessed to the murder. He had been taken home.

At lunchtime on Wednesday David Tanner was sitting in the Red Lion pub in Skipton, trying to figure out how he'd come to this point in his life. He'd joined the Secret Service at the age of 22. He was now 39 years of age. He'd been well thought of as an MI5 field operative and had gained much kudos by being seconded to MI6. His time in Iraq had been successful until he found out about Michael Maxim's little sideline, rare artefacts. Most were only worth thousands, but one was worth millions. Stupidly, Tanner had turned a blind eye. For him it was crucial for the SAS team to succeed in its covert operations and Maxim had been central to that success. When he found out that Maxim had smuggled out a pure-gold crafted chariot and horse, only the size of a child's small toy, so delicate yet so perfect, and over three thousand years old, one of the greatest treasures of Iraqi art, he knew that Maxim had to be stopped. He'd informed his masters in London who were suspicious of his own involvement. They were both recalled but the chariot had 'disappeared', with Maxim denying everything. MI5 had continued to use the SAS man but after he had crossed into Eire without authorisation, resulting in the death of an officer of the Garda, they had decided that he must be terminated. The task had been given to Tanner and two junior officers. Tanner had realized that he was being tested. When the three MI5 officers had entered the safe house to meet Maxim and his son, on the pretence of setting up another operation, Michael Maxim had been ready. Even with his bouts of drinking he understood when he was being set up. He had shot two of them as they entered the room, with Jonathan Maxim, armed only with a knife, standing behind his father. To his own shame David Tanner had run for his life, rationalising his own behaviour later with 'better to live to fight another day'. MI5 had not fully believed his telling of events and soon took the decision to demote him. He had been sent to a desk job in Catterick of all places. Tanner was desperate to resurrect his career as an agent in the field, but he was hurting badly. Peter Wilson had been a good colleague and an even better friend. He wasn't supposed to end up dead!

Tanner finished a third glass of whisky and got himself another. He knew, or he thought he knew, that Sally Henshaw was the daughter of Michael Maxim and that near harmless sleepy Cray, in an idyllic cottage, there were two very dangerous men. He could tell the police and it would all be over, but he would still be in Catterick behind a desk and Maxim would probably get the chance to sing like a canary in court. He could deal with Maxim himself and be back, back with MI5 in London, back where he wanted to be, or he could be dead!

Late that evening, Sally Henshaw rang her brother.

'Hello gorgeous boy. Have you made all the arrangements for Amsterdam?'

'Yes, Sal.'

'And you've moved all the money?'

'Yes, Sal. What do we do about the toy?'

'It was father's, Jonny. You decide.'

'OK, Sis. Goodnight, sleep well.'

She didn't. She knew that they were closing in.

THURSDAY SECOND WEEK IN JULY

Helen Warren believed that today was going to be very important to her. She was using her own initiative and desperately trying to make a difference in the investigation of Peter Wilson's death. And, yes, she wanted to be noticed by the higher-ups!

Throughout the morning she searched for six pubs between Market Tatton and Lowestoft and straightforwardly found the first four, being situated on the main road. They were modern, professionally run and obviously successful, bringing in lots of locals and middle-class holidaymakers to enjoy the Broads. However, her questions were greeted universally with the shaking of heads. The fifth pub on her list proved more difficult to find. She had to leave the main route to Lowestoft and follow a series of increasingly minor roads until, after being lost for over an hour, she eventually ended up at a no-through-road sign. Beyond it, about a hundred yards down a track only wide enough for one car, she could see a pub sign. Boaters Inn, beside a little visited backwater of the Broads, had seen better days. It needed a new paint job and obvious repairs to old casement windows with tired green shutters. As Helen parked the BMW on a grassed area in front of the pub, dotted with damaged picnic tables, she mused that it had probably closed, but she was wrong. There was a solitary drinker sat outside near the entrance. She nodded at the old man as she went in. At the bar was a young confident-looking woman. Helen took her identification card from her pocket and held it up for inspection. The woman just smiled.

'What can I do for you, officer, or is it detective?' she asked. 'I do hope you'd like a drink of something.'

'Certainly,' replied PC Warren,' a coke and ice, please. I'm making enquiries in the area about a Mrs Elaine Law who lived in Market Tatton twenty or thirty years ago.'

The woman laughed out loud.

'How old do you think I am!' she exclaimed. 'Try asking my grandfather. He's sitting outside having his mid-morning pint.'

She came out from behind the bar and walked outside into the sunshine. The old man, eighty-five if a day, downed the rest of his drink and looked up at Helen Warren from beneath massive grey eyebrows.

'I heard what you said in there, young lady, but first, thank you, yes, I would like another pint.'

He offered Helen his glass. She looked across at the granddaughter and nodded with a smile. He continued.

'I may be old and senile but, unlike my beautiful granddaughter here, who seems to have forgotten her Auntie Elly, I remember Elaine Law very well. She used to visit here a lot when you were little, Sandy.'

He shook his head at his granddaughter.

'Oh, you mean Sally's mum!' Sandy shouted.

'Can I ask you your name, sir?' asked Helen.

'Barton,' said the old man, 'and this is my granddaughter, beautiful but unmarried, Miss Alexandra Roberts, now owner of this fine loss-making pub.'

'And her mother, your daughter?'

'Sadly, she passed away,' came the quiet reply.

'Oh, sorry sir. And do either of you know the name, Maxim?' asked Helen.

Both shook their heads. Helen was somewhat crestfallen. It hadn't been two Sallys after all. Mrs Dean had mis-remembered. Nevertheless, she persisted.

'Did you lose touch with Mrs Law and Sally after they moved to London? That must have been when you were about ten, Miss Roberts?'

The old man interjected.

'You obviously don't know, lady policeman,' he said sombrely.

'Oh my God, yes,' added Sandy.

Helen held her breath. The old man continued.

'The family did move to London, a new start for the three of them. I remember Elaine being so excited. Shortly after they got there, they went on a family holiday to Tuscany. Wiped out in a car accident, the whole lot!'

'Good God!' exclaimed Helen. 'You are certain, sir? Do you know about the funeral?'

'Of course, I'm certain,' said the old man. 'Sandy's mum was so upset. The funeral was out in Italy. Elaine had always wanted to go, so they were buried out there. Awful it was! My daughter flew out. I stayed here with Sandy.'

'I'm so sorry to have had to bring back such memories,' PC Warren said sympathetically. 'If you excuse me for a minute, I just need to make a phone call, then let me buy you both a drink.'

She walked to the car and sat in the front seat talking to DS Trueman over the phone, then returned to the old man and his granddaughter. It was 3.35 p.m.

At 3 o'clock PC Craven and David Tanner were due to meet with Superintendent Blair and DI Tate. At ten past three a very nervous Craven was sat alone opposite his two senior colleagues.

'I'm sorry, sir, I don't know where Mr Tanner is. I've been trying his mobile for the last two hours but no reply. I haven't seen him since Tuesday afternoon. He seemed very distracted and left the office early. He didn't come in yesterday.'

Tate rolled his eyes at Blair.

'Do you know what he's up to, Constable Craven?' asked Tate.

'No, sir, but he'd spoken to Andrew Wilson. Maybe it upset him.'

'Doubtful!' retorted Blair. 'What did Andrew Wilson want?'

'I don't know, sir. Just to be re-assured, I think Mr Tanner said.'

Blair swore under his breath. Tate spoke with severity.

'Go to the Wilson house, constable, now. Find out what Andrew Wilson told Tanner. It could be important. Phone me as soon as you know anything. Now, constable!'

Craven jumped to his feet and was gone.

At 3.50 p.m. DS Trueman knocked and entered Blair's office. He spoke breathlessly.

'Helen Warren has been told by a man who knew the Laws in Market Tatton that Mrs Elaine Law, her husband, and Sally Law, were all killed in a motoring accident in Italy nearly twenty years ago. We're trying to confirm. It looks like their lives subsequently have been manufactured digitally by someone. It can be done if you're a good enough hacker.'

'Bugger!' exclaimed Blair. 'Tanner was right, and I'll guess he knows he was.'

'He might have chosen not to tell us. He's got his own agenda,' added Tate.

Tate's mobile phone rang. He answered and listened intently to what Craven had to tell him. Blair and Trueman observed Tate in silence. After what seemed to be an age, but was only a matter of two minutes, Tate put down his phone and looked directly at Blair.

'Sally Henshaw lied to us about getting a bus to Skipton on the Monday morning when the car was discovered in Hawes. She was seen in Hawes by Andrew Wilson, standing at a bus stop. She must have driven the car there herself. At the very least she's been part of a cover up.'

'So,' said Blair, 'Sally Henshaw is Michael Maxim's daughter, and her father and brother may still be at Scargill Cottage. I wonder how much poor Peter Wilson actually knew or whether he just stumbled into it.'

Another phone rang. This time it was DS Trueman's. He answered it and listened.

'Italian authorities have just confirmed the deaths of the Law family in a car accident near Florence.'

'We need an armed response team if we go up to the cottage, sir,' said Tate.

'Yes, Inspector, but this is Skipton, not London. I must speak to the Assistant Chief Constable. We need help. This is dangerous and I hope to God they've gone. Just in case, see if we can put a squad together. I'll talk to the ACC.'

Tate and Trueman left the office. Blair phoned ACC Harris and explained the full situation. Harris was not an action man, he was a police administrator and insisted on consulting the Chief Constable. At 4.30 Tate came back into the office.

'We have six armed officers, sir, including Trueman and myself, all trained men but with very little experience in a situation like this. What does the ACC say?'

'Bugger all use, Alan. He's talking to the Chief Constable. We wait.'

Tate kicked his chair and then apologised.

At five o'clock Blair's phone sprang into life. It was Harris who spoke in a formal 'I'm your superior' voice.

'The Chief Constable and I feel that there is insufficient cause to request an armed response from outside North Yorkshire. You are to deal with the matter yourself but must proceed with due caution.'

Blair tried to argue but was silenced immediately. With a 'Yes, sir' he slammed down the phone and uttered an oath even DI Tate had never heard him utter.

'All down to us, Alan. First, though, we need information from Sally Henshaw if she's still there at The Inn. I'll go with Craven. You take armed response up to Scargill Cottage, quietly. Set up a perimeter and then wait. Just observe. No shooting unless you have no choice. Use your own judgement. You have my full confidence.'

'Thank you, sir. But where the hell is Tanner?'

'Frankly, DI Tate, I don't much care, so long as he doesn't get in our way. Brief the full team including medics on the layout of the cottage and surroundings. Use Craven, he's been up there. If we're ready, we go at seven, but remember, quietly, we don't want to scare half of Wharfedale.'

At seven fifteen, two unmarked Range Rovers and two cars, including Blair's own Jaguar, set off at rapid speed from Skipton police station. Less than thirty minutes later they arrived in the tiny hamlet of Buckden and came to a halt a hundred yards short of The Inn.

'Right, Alan,' said Blair, 'head up to the cottage. Establish a perimeter far enough away so as not to be spotted. We're just observing until we know more. We're not going through any doors. This isn't television. There might only be a little old lady in there, but there could be two fully trained killers, one ex-SAS, with more expertise than we'll ever have! I'll try to find out what we face from Sally Henshaw. Otherwise, Craven and I will join you as quickly as we can. Good luck.'

Tate got out of the Jaguar and into the car behind. The three police vehicles set off slowly past The Inn before accelerating away towards Cray.

'Right, let's go,' said Blair to Craven. Both men were in uniform. They walked slowly along the road to the entrance of the pub. The door was shut, and they could hear no noise from inside. A voice from behind, across the road, shouted to them.

'The pub's been closed all day, officers. Bit strange for a Thursday evening.'

It was a helpful local. Neither of them replied.

Craven tried the door. It was locked. They walked round the side of the pub into the car park. There was a landrover and a hatchback which Craven recognised as the Henshaw's. He tried the back-door entrance and pushed it open. He could hear no voices, no movement. Blair signalled to Craven not to speak and they checked the bar, the restaurant, and the kitchen. Craven pointed a finger upwards and slowly made his way up the main stair followed by Blair, both filled with apprehension. They found nothing until, finally, Craven pushed open the door to the main bedroom. Lying on the floor, tied and gagged, and still unconscious, was Tom Henshaw, with purple bruising to the side of his neck. Craven checked his breathing, cut the plastic wrist ties and removed the gag. He put him in the recovery position and then tried to bring him round gently.

'He'll be OK, sir, I think,' said Craven.

Blair was already on his mobile phone.

'Ambulance to The Inn, Buckden, immediately. Man unconscious, in a bad way,' he barked.

'You stay here with him, Craven. The ambulance should be here within fifteen minutes. See if you can get him conscious. I'm going up to Scargill Cottage. I'll guess that this is Tanner's work. What the hell is the fool up to?'

Blair phoned Tate as he walked swiftly back to the Jaguar.

'Agreed, Alan,' he said. 'Tanner might be on a one-man operation. With you in five minutes.'

In the distance, a church bell chimed eight o'clock as Blair noiselessly parked his car behind one of the Range Rovers, some fifty yards before the conifer screen entrance to Scargill Cottage's tarmac drive. It would be dark in just under three hours.

At four o'clock on that Thursday afternoon, David Tanner placed his automatic pistol into his shoulder holster and tapped it three times for luck, something he'd done ever since the debacle at the safe house. He had a pocket full of plastic ties, just like those used by the average gardener, but carried no other weapons. He hated knives, 'useful but too messy' he had once said jokingly to Michael Maxim.

He left his Skipton hotel and drove north. It was an idyllic summer's day, but he saw none of that. His mind was concentrating now, his plan was set. The funniest joke would have been incapable of raising a smile. He was picturing the situations ahead, like a rehearsal, and he must get his lines spot on.

At around five o'clock he parked his car behind The Inn, next to the Henshaw's landrover, and entered the pub through the open back entrance. The previous day he had phoned and discovered that it didn't open until six o'clock. He could hear someone moving around upstairs. First, he checked downstairs. There was no-one. He silently climbed the main stair to the first floor. He had familiarised himself with the pub layout when he stayed there days before. He walked along the landing to the master bedroom and knocked quietly. Tom Henshaw opened the door, expecting to see his wife. The rather shocked landlord said:

'What on earth are you doing here, Mr Tanner? Need to book in?'

Tanner lifted his right hand in an instant and dealt a savage blow to the left side of the landlord's neck. He fell, with Tanner cradling him to the floor and dragging him back into his own bedroom. He checked his pulse. 'You'll live,' he thought. He tied his wrists and feet together with four plastic ties, before gagging him. He left the bedroom, quietly closing the door behind him. He stood stock still and listened intently. Where was Sally Henshaw! He needed her if he was to get into Scargill Cottage. It was then that he heard a car door slam. Sally had returned from shopping in Kettlewell. He rushed downstairs to the bar and sat down at a table next to the window.

'Hello!' he shouted. 'Any chance of a drink? I'm in the bar.'

'We don't open 'til six,' came the reply as Sally walked in.

'Take a seat, Mrs Henshaw, or is it Sally Maxim?'

Tanner was pointing his gun at her.

'You don't seem shocked,' he continued.

'No, I know who you are, Mr Tanner. You're MI5. I saw you years ago, running for your life. Where's Tom?'

'Sleeping upstairs. He'll be fine,' said Tanner, disturbed by her calmness and the fact that she must have seen him at the safe house.

'What do you want?' she asked, with obvious distaste.

'Your father, your brother, maybe even you.'

'You're mad. If you're on your own, you can't have told the police who I am. You've got no chance!'

'Alive or dead, it doesn't matter to me, that's your choice. I know they're up there at the cottage. You're going to get me in. From your point of view, it's your best chance. Otherwise, it's the police.'

'But why are you doing this? Why haven't you told the police?'

'That's my business. Let's just say that your father was my responsibility and he's alive when he shouldn't be. And Peter Wilson was my friend.'

Sally laughed.

'You idiot. All ego and revenge, just another macho fool. You're going to die, Tanner!'

He moved towards her at speed and pressed the barrel of the automatic against her cheek. He pushed her face down onto a table, put down the gun and held her wrists together behind her back with one hand. With the other he tied them together with two plastic ties. She swore at him but was powerless to stop him. He grabbed his gun and moved back. As she stood, he motioned her towards the back door. She softened her voice.

'My father's dead.'

'Do you think I'm stupid?' he shouted back, pointing the gun at her head.

'He is! Four years ago. He'd had too much to drink one night and started slapping me around when I took the glass away from him. Jonny grabbed him to protect me, he always protects me, but father wouldn't stop. He kept punching Jonny's face. Jonny screamed at him to stop. He was crying and then, out of nowhere, he hit father. One blow to the throat, that's all it took.'

Sally Henshaw was crying real tears now, and Tanner knew it.

'If I believe you, tell me, what did you do with your father's body?'

'We buried it in the wood next to the cottage.'

Light dawned on Tanner.

'Ah, that cross,' he said, shaking his head, 'I saw it. Hell, I thought someone had buried a dog. Stupid! But if your father's dead then there's still your brother up there to deal with!'

'No, Jonny left over a year ago. There's only mother up at the cottage.'

Tanner laughed.

'Your mother, eh! Too smart Mrs Henshaw. Remember, I've been up to Scargill Cottage with the police. I've met your mother and I saw her charge off the day before in her SUV.'

'So?' she replied.

Tanner laughed again, pacing left and right, his gun still pointing towards her.

'If your brother left a year ago, how come his DNA was up on Mastiles Lane when we found Peter Wilson?'

Her face fell.

'My brother didn't mean to kill him,' she pleaded. 'Wilson had a gun. He would have killed Jonny.'

'Peter Wilson hardly knew how to use a gun!' Tanner spat back at her. 'Enough of this. Outside! And, if you want your brother to live, when we get up there, do exactly what I say.'

It went through Tanner's mind that now was the time to tell the police everything, but he'd come too far to stop. He pushed Sally onto the back seat of his car and drove at rapid speed up the main road to Cray. He climbed the hill and turned right for the cottage. He drove slowly between the screen of conifers. The cottage, and half a dozen security cameras, were only two hundred yards away. He stopped the car and got out fast, assuming he would have already been seen. He pulled his captive out of the back and held her from behind by her golden hair, twisted in his left hand, with his automatic in the right, pointed at her temple. The two of them moved slowly in a straight line towards the garden gate. Suddenly, the cottage front door began to open. Tanner stared at it, but no-one could be seen. It was an invitation, almost like a childish dare, to come in.

'Come out here, Maxim,' shouted Tanner. There was no reply.

'Tell him to come out,' he said to Sally.

'No, Mr Tanner,' she stated with finality.

Slowly, Tanner pushed her through the door, all the time holding the gun against her cheek, staring into semi-darkness. He blinked and his vision cleared. Standing in the middle of the room was Jonathan Maxim, hands by his side, wearing a black dress, bright red lipstick and a dark purple wig. He smiled and, unnervingly for Tanner, seemed relaxed.

'You must be a very brave or a very stupid man, Mr Tanner,' he said softly. 'You're hurting my sister, and I don't like that, and mother doesn't like that, does she Sal?'

'No, she doesn't, gorgeous boy,' she said calmly.

Tanner fixed his gaze on Jonathan Maxim. Suddenly, he pushed Sally away to the right and held the automatic in a two-handed grip aimed directly at Maxim's head.

'You can't just shoot me, Mr Tanner. You're one of the good guys. But then, I only kill those who threaten me, whereas you, Mr Tanner, well, we've met before and you tried to kill father and me then, and two of your men are dead. You really shouldn't be trying to kill me again.'

'I'm not going to kill you Maxim, I'm going to take you in, for the murder of Peter Wilson.'

'But mother wouldn't like that,' said Maxim.

Tanner smiled back at him.

'No, she wouldn't,' came a voice from behind him.

Tanner whipped round and instinctively fired his automatic at the same time as Maxim's mother pulled the trigger of Peter Wilson's gun that she'd picked up and hidden days ago. Her bullet smacked into the ceiling. In that same instant, Jonathan Maxim pulled a knife from the sleeve of his dress and hurled it towards Tanner. The old lady fell to the floor, dead. Tanner turned to be hit by a thunderous fist to his face and crumpled in a heap next to her. Maxim kicked him in the head for good measure and got down on his knees next to his mother. He started to howl.

'Get my hands free, Jonny!' shouted his sister. 'Mother's dead!'

He pulled the knife from Tanner's back, just below his left shoulder and cut the plastic ties. Sally rubbed her wrists vigorously.

'There's nothing we can do about mother. She's gone!' she said calmly. 'We've got to get out of here. The police could come at any time.'

'But what are we going to do with mother?' he pleaded, 'And, I don't think Tanner's dead. Should I kill him, Sal?'

'No, Jonny. I've had enough of this. We've got to go but we can bury mother with father, if you want, and say a prayer.'

'That would be nice,' he replied, childlike again. 'Can I stay dressed up?' he asked.

'Of course,' she replied, kissing his forehead.

They tied Tanner's hands and feet together and then carried mother's body, in a sheet, out into the wood close by. Sally removed the small wooden cross and Jonny dug a shallow grave next to Michael Maxim's. They gently placed the body in the grave and covered it with earth. Sally replaced the wooden cross and said a short prayer while Jonny wept.

'That was nice,' he said as they walked back into the cottage.

'Now, Jonny, have you done everything as I asked? The route, tickets, ferry, all on your laptop?'

'Yes, just as you asked, Sal, but I've made it harder.'

'Good,' she said, smiling. 'Carry the bags to the SUV. Let's go.'

The brother and sister walked swiftly to the car, drove down the drive and turned right. Three minutes later they were at Scargill Farm, met by a very confused Fred Denby, who stared at Jonathan Maxim.

'Hello, Jon, you look amazingly like your mother,' he said, trying not to laugh. 'Nice to see you again, Mrs Henshaw. As beautiful as ever!'

'We need your car, Mr Denby, and we need you to keep our SUV in your farm buildings, out of sight, for a week, say, and then you can find it, if you know what I mean.'

The farmer saw the pistol in Sally Henshaw's right hand.

'We will make it worth your while, Mr Denby, but you must promise to say nothing for one week. Is twenty-five thousand pounds sufficient?'

'You have a deal, Mrs Henshaw!'

The slightly drunk farmer spat on his right palm and shook hands with her. She handed him an envelope while Jonny drove the SUV into the nearest building. Denby went into the farmhouse and returned with the keys to his car.

Tate aimed his binoculars at each window of Scargill Cottage, in turn, but saw no sign of life. The car standing halfway down the driveway, with two doors wide open, he didn't recognise. He reasoned that Tanner had come up here with Sally Henshaw, but when, and who if anyone, was inside the cottage? Blair was standing behind him, mobile phone clamped to his right ear. The call ended.

'That was Craven. Tom Henshaw's on his way to hospital. The paramedics brought him round and he's going to be OK. He confirmed it was Tanner who knocked him out, but hours ago. Whatever's happened up here, it should be over by now. Craven said there should be a black SUV parked out front, and that's gone. We go in, now.'

Tate signalled to four officers clad in black, carrying automatic weapons, hidden in the wood to the side of the cottage. They moved at rapid speed along the front of the cottage, ducking under windows. The first two officers smashed open the front door and the second two were in. No more than thirty seconds had elapsed. Tate's head set sprang into life.

'In sir, man down, it's Tanner. Checking rest of cottage.'

'All rooms empty. Checking rear buildings.'

'All buildings empty. Need medics.'

Tate shouted, 'Medics in, now, man down,' and two men rushed into the cottage.

Tanner had been lucky. He was still alive. The knife had missed anything vital, though he was finding it difficult to breathe and had lost a lot of blood. One medic gave him a morphine injection while the other patched the wound. Tanner was barely conscious and severely concussed. Fifteen minutes later he was in the back of a blue light ambulance, screaming through Cray.

Tate put out a nationwide alert to track down the black SUV and instructed his men to search the area around the cottage. With Trueman and Craven, who had rushed up from Buckden, he entered the cottage with Superintendent Blair.

'OK, gentlemen,' said Blair, 'let's try to figure out what's gone on here. Search everywhere. Craven, you're good with the IT. See what's around.'

''I'll check that room, sir,' he said, pointing through the kitchen to an open door, 'it might be the office.'

Craven walked into Jonathan Maxim's bedroom to see an array of IT equipment on desks against the wall opposite, including a laptop that had been left running, with a screensaver consisting of a smiling policeman. In front of the laptop was a clear Perspex box. Inside the box was the most beautiful object that Craven had ever seen. It was a gold war chariot. On top of the box was a scribbled note which read: 'Please return to owner. Kind regards, Jonathan.'

'DI Tate,' he shouted, 'you'd better see this, sir.'

The three other officers hurried into the room and fixed their eyes on the box. Craven read the note out loud.

'What exactly is that?' asked Trueman.

'Well,' said Blair, 'I've seen something very like it in the British Museum, Persian or Egyptian perhaps, and worth millions. If Maxim knows what it is, and he's giving it away, he's either mad or rich or both!'

'Try the laptop,' said Tate. 'I suggest from the screensaver that someone is playing with us.'

Craven clicked on 'sign in', expecting nothing. The smiling policeman waved goodbye and was replaced by a question, which read:

'If I go halfway from Halifax to Norwich what am I getting? Bye bye!'

Luckily, Craven quickly wrote down the question as Blair swore at the laptop when, thirty seconds later, the question disappeared.

'Interrogate that bloody laptop, Craven,' said Blair, 'that lunatic wants to play games. And if you can answer that question, get back to me!' With that he stormed out of the room. Tate smiled at Trueman, with, 'Not pleased, not pleased at all.' They then left Craven to it, returning to search the rest of the cottage.

An officer rushed through the front door and shouted to Tate:

'Sir, we've found a body, and maybe another, in the wood.'

Tate and Blair followed the young constable to find two other officers standing over a dead body, while a third was digging the ground next to a wooden cross.

'Well, that must be Mrs Law, or Maxim,' offered Tate. 'I wonder how she ended up dead?'

Just then, the officer who was digging, recoiled at what he had found. It was a very decomposed body, smiling up at him.

'Who the hell is that?' said Tate. 'It must have been here years.'

'We've got problems, Alan,' said Blair. 'I hope to God that Tanner knows more than we do!'

Tate phoned Skipton to send forensics and more manpower, and lights. It was going to be a long night. As they returned to the cottage, Craven came through the kitchen.

Sir,' he said to DI Tate, 'The other computers were all password protected, but the laptop wasn't. It seems to have been set up for us, just like a game. Jonathan Maxim left a spreadsheet listing one hundred possible journeys, by plane, ferry and train, from multiple airports and terminals, to five separate destinations on the continent. All tomorrow, sir, but there are no details of tickets or providers.'

'Jesus,' said Tate, 'this man is severely disturbed!'

'Yes,' responded Blair, 'disturbed, dangerous and bloody clever! What's our best guess, that Michael Maxim, his son and daughter, are leaving the country tomorrow, or are we just being set up? Put out descriptions, Alan, as best we can, and let's find that SUV. Notify all ports, etcetera.'

Well before the sun finally set on that mid-summer's day, Jonathan Maxim and his sister were a hundred miles away in a small twin-bedded room in a modest hotel, after discarding farmer Denby's car in a long-term multi-storey car park. Jonathan was now dressed in casual men's clothing and was sitting on his bed examining the dinner menu. He was famished.

'How are you getting on, Sal?' he shouted in the direction of the bathroom, trying to overcome the noise. The hair dryer fell silent and Sally Henshaw emerged, goddess-like.

'What do you think?' she asked. He stared up at her.

'You look great, Sis. Black hair really suits you.'

FRIDAY SECOND WEEK IN JULY

Superintendent Blair was about to have one last check of his emails before going to bed when headlights lit up the living room curtains as a police car pulled up outside his substantial detached house in Grassington. He opened the front door to see an agitated DI Tate.

'Sorry to disturb you, sir, but I feel we need to talk before morning.'

'Come on through, Alan,' said Blair.

The two seated themselves at the polished dining room table. Still up after midnight, and in her dressing gown, Blair's very understanding wife, who had seen it all before over the years, brought through two cups of coffee and a plateful of ginger biscuits.

'I've been at the hospital. They sorted Tanner's wound out as soon as he was admitted. He's back in a private ward now. He'll be OK. He's been conscious for the last hour or so and has given us his version of events.'

'Carry on, Alan,' said Blair, sipping on his coffee.

'Tanner did knock out Tom Henshaw. He said it was safer than pulling a gun on him. He'd figured out that his wife was Maxim's daughter and forcibly took her up to Scargill Cottage. Before they'd left Buckden, she told him that

Michael Maxim was already dead, killed by his son. Self-defence, she claims. He's the other body in the wood.'

'So why the hell did Tanner go up there on his own and not get police backup?'

Blair was angry, but angry with the wrong person.

'He was vague on that, sir. He says he used Sally Henshaw to get in the cottage and had Jonathan Maxim at gunpoint when his mother shot at him and missed. He shot Mrs Law, but Maxim dealt with him with a knife and a kick to the head. For some reason, Maxim didn't finish him off. He's no idea what happened after that, but it means that only two are on the run. And there's another strange thing, sir. Jonathan Maxim was dressed as a woman. He looked just like his own mother.'

Blair was thinking fast.

'This is problematic, Alan. I'm not sure what nationwide resources can be put to this. Michael Maxim is a known wanted killer but he's dead. Jonathan Maxim is dangerous, we know that, but he was confronted by Tanner with a gun and responded as you might expect when Tanner killed his mother. And we're still uncertain about how Peter Wilson met his death. According to the pathologist, he may have killed himself accidently with his own gun. The Chief Constable won't be too happy if we disrupt a hundred crossings to the continent because we believe that someone whose mother was shot by an MI5 agent is dangerous!'

'Agreed, sir. That's why I thought I'd better tell you tonight. There is something else though, sir. It might be a red herring, but Craven reckons he can answer Maxim's laptop question.'

'Really!' exclaimed Blair. 'Go on, enlighten me.'

'Well, sir, apparently Craven likes crosswords. He suggests that 'If I go from Halifax to Norwich' could mean take HA from Halifax and put it with RWICH from Norwich to get.'

'Harwich!' exclaimed Blair. 'To get a ferry from Harwich! Any match with that list on Maxim's laptop?'

'Oh yes, sir,' said Tate. 'The ferry across to the Netherlands at midday.'

Blair slammed his fist down on the table.

'It's worth a gamble and it's the only one we've got!'

At seven in the morning, Blair attempted to persuade a suddenly awake Assistant Chief Constable to put out a nationwide alert to stop Jonathan Maxim and Sally Henshaw leaving the country. The police did have a current photograph of Mrs Henshaw, but only a ten-year out of date one of her brother. When asked by the ACC whether he had actual proof that Jonathan Maxim was a murderer, Blair said truthfully that he did not. Their discussion ended abruptly.

Soon after, Craven drove away from Skipton police station in the unmarked Jaguar, carrying Blair, Tate and Trueman.

'Step on it,' said Blair. 'I suggest we get to Harwich before twelve!'

'Yes, sir,' replied Craven, smiling to himself.

At eight o'clock, Sally Henshaw and her brother left their hotel carrying hand luggage only and walked the short distance to the station. As the train started its journey south, Jonathan turned to his sister and said:

'If I ever see Tanner again, I'll kill him, Sal.'

He started to weep.

'No, you won't, Jonny,' she said. 'Mother's with father now. Everything's alright.'

'Yes,' he replied, 'everything's alright.'

According to Craven's route planner it should have taken just under five hours to get to Harwich ferry terminal. He screamed down the A1, and then across country south of

Cambridge, to arrive at twenty minutes to midday. He enjoyed driving Blair's Jaguar.

'Nice drive, Mark,' said Trueman to Craven, as the two more senior officers got out of the car and walked over to a man clearly waiting for them. The man reached out to shake hands with DI Tate.

'Nice to see you in these parts, Alan,' he said.

Tate introduced DI Proud to Superintendent Blair.

'We have two armed plain clothes officers here, sir, one at the vehicle entry point, one at pedestrian entry, and I've supplied them with descriptions of the two you're after. There are also two more armed uniformed officers, positioned discreetly close by. Terminal staff have been forewarned and given names and the SUV number to look out for. No sign of them yet, sir, and most passengers and vehicles are already on board.'

'Good job, Detective Inspector,' responded Blair. 'but I'm guessing that they'll get aboard separately on foot, with false documents and disguises, I should think. Craven knows Mrs Henshaw well though. I suggest we check the passenger lounges just before the ship sails.

'We'd better have a decent lunch, Jonny,' Sally Henshaw said to her brother. 'It'll be almost four hours to get across.'

They were sat at a small table, with their bags at their feet, in the lounge bar, observing the chaos around them, as ferry passengers settled aboard, ready to queue at the cafeteria for food and drink.

'OK, Sal,' came the reply. 'Ham, egg and chips, please. I'll just sit here and stare out of the window. I like being on a ferry.'

Sally smiled at her brother.

At midday, Proud, Blair, Tate and Craven boarded the Harwich ferry. Both Proud and Tate were armed. Craven led the way with eyes dancing from side to side, searching as they walked purposefully through the passenger lounges. Most passengers were seated now, and ready to depart. At the far side of the lounge bar, he spotted the golden hair of a woman, seated with her back to him. He froze and then pointed across, before slowly following Tate and Proud, with Blair bringing up the rear. Tate tapped the woman on the shoulder. She turned and looked up at him.

'Yes?' she said.

148

Tate glanced at Craven who shook his head.

Forty minutes later, after a full but fruitless search, the ferry set sail once Superintendent Blair had apologised profusely to the Captain for the delay.

As the Jaguar left Harwich on its long journey back north, Tate turned to Blair to offer consolation.

'It was worth a try, sir. We couldn't cover a hundred departures. They may be getting away today, or it could just be a diversion. Maybe they'll go to ground again.'

Blair was an unhappy man.

'Yes, it was worth a try, but I can't help but feel that we've been toyed with. And that hurts. They'll be well away from our patch by now, but where? That's somebody else's problem. You can slow to normal speeds, Craven. We're not in a hurry.'

Jonathan Maxim marvelled at what he saw out of the ferry window.

'Look at all those wind turbines. There must be a hundred!'

Then he added:

'I wonder if the police are having a good day?' He burst out laughing. 'I wonder if they went on a day trip to Harwich?' He continued in fits of laughter. 'When I made up my game on the laptop, I knew you must have already figured out what to do. You always do. You were trying to trick me, Sal, like when we were little.'

Sally Henshaw smiled and tousled her brother's hair.

'Yes, Jonny. You do love your games. I knew you'd give them a clue, and that was too dangerous for us.'

'And that's why you told me to send the money to Dougie, isn't it?'

'Yes,' she replied, almost sternly.

'Well, I'm really looking forward to seeing Dougie. We haven't been, together, since that holiday with mother when we were about twelve.'

'I knew you'd be pleased,' she said. 'And I've got us a very nice house.'

They both stopped talking and focussed on their food, every now and then staring out of the huge window at England disappearing in the distance.

Late on that Friday afternoon, the brother and sister disembarked. They had arrived at Douglas, on the Isle of Man.

SATURDAY THIRD WEEK IN JULY

After spending all morning picking horses, with cups of tea, a pen, and the Racing Post, Fred Denby settled down in front of the television to watch Saturday afternoon racing. The first race had just got underway when the phone in the hallway rang. He swore.

'Fred Denby speaking,' he said to the caller, sharply.

'Hello, Mr Denby. This is Carlisle police. Do you own a green Rover, registered in 2004, sir?'

'You obviously know I do, young man, otherwise you wouldn't be disturbing me in the middle of a race on a Saturday.'

'Yes, sir. Well, we've found it.'

'Found it? It should be in my garage,' replied the farmer, feigning ignorance. 'Let me go check. Phone me back in five minutes.'

With that, he rushed through to the living room to see DanceIntoTheLight flash by the winning post. He clapped his hands with a 'well done my beauty' and sat back down. When the phone rang again, he tried to sound very concerned.

'Well, young man, you won't believe this, but my car's gone, and I've discovered a much newer one in my shed, a black SUV. It looks like the one at Scargill Cottage next door to me, where there's been all that trouble according to this morning's paper.'

The young constable on the end of the phone excitedly took down all details. He promised to see that the farmer's car was returned to him and said that Skipton police would be in touch very shortly. After the call, Fred returned to his television set, hoping that the police didn't arrive until after the last race.

Two hours later DS Trueman and PC Craven were examining the SUV.

'It's definitely Mrs Law's. They must have hidden it here and stolen Mr Denby's Rover.'

'Yes, it looks that way,' said Trueman, glancing suspiciously over at the farmer.

Craven took a statement from Denby, while Trueman set off back to Skipton in the SUV. On arrival at the police station he was met by an annoyed DI Tate.

'So, while we were concentrating on exits to the continent, south and east, they were heading north to Carlisle. Where to after that, eh?'

Tate was kicking the ground next to the SUV, hands in pockets.

'Carlisle, sir. Quick train to London for Eurostar or Heathrow, or an easy drive across to Stranraer for the Belfast ferry, or up to Glasgow, or.'

'Yes, yes, sergeant, you've made your point! Anyway, as Blair says, it's not our problem now.'

SUNDAY THIRD WEEK IN JULY

Tom Henshaw had finished his hospital breakfast and was now fully dressed, sitting by the side of his bed reading the Sunday paper. The headline on page four was 'Killing in Wharfedale'. He read through the article, full of half-truths and speculation. The police had put out a very brief press release. All he got from it was that Sally's mother had been killed by person or persons unknown and that police were searching for Mr Jonathan Maxim and Mrs Sally Henshaw in connection with the death. There was a picture of Sally.

'Where did they get that from?' Tom thought to himself.

Physically, he had recovered very quickly, and had been given the go ahead to go home after lunch, but, mentally, he was a wreck. The police had interviewed him at length the previous day, much to the annoyance of hospital staff, but had soon realized that he knew very little about the goings on at Scargill Cottage. He hadn't even known that Sally had a brother! He had become very angry when interviewed. Things that were implied about his wife! To Tom Henshaw, Sally was the best thing in his life, and she was gone!

'It wasn't my wife who put me in hospital, it was that bloody maniac Tanner. There'll be hell to pay for this. I'm going to press charges,' he had barked at DI Tate.

154

Tate hadn't told him that Tanner was only three doors away, in a private room, or that he was recovering well after being stabbed and battered by his own wife's brother. It would be mid-week before the MI5 officer was released from hospital.

By mid-afternoon, Tom Henshaw was back in The Inn, furnished with three sorts of pills to take over the following seven days. The previous day, when Tate had mentioned victim support, he had told him to 'sod off'. He sat in a chair all afternoon, staring at the living room walls, drinking whisky, with all doors locked. Suddenly, he began to cry.

'Oh Sal,' he sobbed, 'please come back. I can't cope without you.'

Whisky and three sorts of pills were not a good mix. He fell into a deep sleep. Hours went by. He awoke to a ringing, in complete darkness. The phone rang and rang. He struggled to his feet and unsteadily walked through to the bar. He lifted the receiver.

'Hello Tom, is that you my darling?'

It was the voice that he longed to hear, and he cried like a baby.

'Don't cry, don't cry,' she implored as tears ran down her own face. 'Don't believe anything that the police tell you. I had to get my brother away to safety. They killed mother and they would have killed Jonathan.'

'When can I see you, Sal? What's going to happen?'

'Don't worry, darling. We will be together again. I will make it happen. Believe me.'

'Oh, Sal, I don't understand any of this. The police have said terrible things. And it's all in the papers.'

'I know,' she said. 'One day I'll tell you everything but not now. You've got to be strong, Tom. For us. I'll get a message to you when things have died down a bit. I love you, darling.'

She put down the phone in her Douglas hotel room and glanced over at Jonny sleeping.

Tom continued to hold his phone, as a talisman. For a few moments, at least, all his fears had been banished from his mind.

WEDNESDAY THIRD WEEK IN JULY

'Sit down, Alan, we need to talk through where we are with the Peter Wilson case. Tanner's out of hospital today, so I've been told.'

'Yes, sir,' said DI Tate, seating himself opposite Superintendent Blair.

'Coffee for you both, sir,' came a voice from behind Tate. Blair's secretary smiled as she left the tray on the large oak desk.

''Well, sir, if I can start us off. I've gone through the pathologist's report again and I tried to get a definitive view from him. He re-stated that, in all probability, Peter Wilson inadvertently shot himself. Certainly, that could have occurred during a scuffle with Jonathan Maxim, but the fact is that Peter Wilson entered Scargill Cottage carrying a weapon. The bullet fired by Mrs Law, according to Tanner, which was found in the ceiling beam, matches the bullet found in Wilson, whose DNA traces have been found inside the cottage. DNA evidence also tells us that Maxim disposed of the body on Mastiles Lane using a quadbike. We have recovered Wilson's gun. Strangely, it was left behind in the cottage, whereas Tanner's automatic is missing. He, of course, after rendering Mr Henshaw unconscious back in Buckden, forced Mrs Henshaw, at gunpoint, to enter the cottage, and then confronted

Jonathan Maxim, before shooting Mrs Law in self-defence, so he claims. The question arises as to who can be charged with what, if ever we catch them. Have I summed things up well for you, sir?'

Blair clasped his hands behind his head and sighed theatrically.

'Rather too well, Alan. You see, I can't help feeling that this is all MI5's fault, or to be more pointed, our good friend Mr Tanner's. MI5 may say that he was acting outside his remit but I'm not sure I buy that. And Peter Wilson had retired, or had he? The secretives, and I include the high-ups, only give us partial truths. MI5 must take responsibility for this mess. They were searching for a murderer, Michael Maxim, but they acted covertly, beyond our realm as police officers. The fact that Michael Maxim had been dead for four years is ironic in the extreme!'

'Yes, sir,' interjected Tate, 'but if I can, respectfully, stick to the point, what could Jonathan Maxim, Sally Henshaw, or David Tanner for that matter, be charged with? What case can we make to the Crown Prosecution Service?'

Blair moved his head slowly from side to side.

'I'll be amazed if the CPS would allow any charges to be brought against Tanner as a serving MI5 officer. His involvement will be glossed over.'

'Tom Henshaw won't like that, sir, an innocent bystander who gets knocked unconscious so that his wife can be abducted.'

'Agreed, Alan, but MI5 might try to suggest that he isn't totally innocent in all this.'

'What about Maxim and Mrs Henshaw? What can we prove? That Jonathan Maxim and Sally Henshaw perverted the course of justice in moving a dead body and an old sportscar! And that they harboured a known murderer! Surely, we can get Maxim for manslaughter, sir?'

'I doubt that, Detective Inspector. Peter Wilson had a gun. As for harbouring a murderer, well, it was their own father and, no doubt, Maxim would claim that his father killed two agents in self-defence. I've also been informed that Jonathan Maxim is a diagnosed schizophrenic.'

'What! How do you know that, sir?'

'Last night, at home, I received a phone call from a secretive, someone higher up than Tanner, who told me more about Maxim than they'd let on before. Apparently, Jonathan Maxim was a brilliant young man. He studied computer science at Cambridge at the age of seventeen, but he didn't fit in. He got bored with the work, finding it too easy. He became withdrawn and started to behave strangely. He left university. Although he received therapy, and was put on permanent antipsychotic medication, his father took him under his wing, in a very

159

negative way, with results as we know, or we think we know.'

Tate asked an obvious question.

'Why did a secretive, as you call them, sir, suddenly decide to ring you up and tell you this?'

'That's a good question, Alan, and I think we both might know the answer. We should find out for definite on Friday. You and I are meeting the aforementioned secretive, with Mr David Tanner, here in my office, at midday.'

'I'm not going to like this, am I sir?'

'No, and neither am I. And do you know what's happened to all Maxim's IT stuff from his room in the cottage?'

'What do you mean, sir? We collected everything and brought it down to Skipton. It's in the evidence room for our techno guys to go through.'

'Not any more, Alan. It's all gone. All gone!'

FRIDAY THIRD WEEK IN JULY

The meeting between Blair and Tate, batting for the police, and Tanner and Dawson, batting for the Secret Service, started off very cordially with handshakes, coffee and general chitchat. Dawson then summed up MI5's perspective. According to him, the whole episode had turned out rather well. Michael Maxim was dead and any sensitive information that he possessed had died with him. MI5 felt that his son was indeed dangerous but that he did not pose a threat to national security in any way. And, as for Sally Henshaw, well, she had mainly been involved as someone supporting her schizophrenic brother. A big plus had been the recovery of the gold war chariot, which would be returned to the people of Iraq, a huge diplomatic coup for the Foreign Office.

Dawson ended his synopsis with, 'I have made the Minister aware of all events and he wishes to convey his personal gratitude to Skipton police, and promises that future funding for this area will be enhanced in next year's spending review.'

Tate sat there fuming, waiting for Blair to explode.

'I'm glad that MI5 are pleased with outcomes,' said Blair, with no hint of irony, 'but I do have several questions and one or two obvious points to make.'

He smiled at Dawson, who did not smile back.

'There's the matter of the two victims in all this. Peter Wilson's family need answers, they need closure, and there's the question of an inquest to be held, even if we accept the tenuous assertion that he accidentally shot himself. And, also, of course, there's Mrs Law, who was shot by Mr Tanner in self-defence.'

'Well,' replied Dawson, 'I can tell you in confidence that Mr Tanner and Mr Wilson were legitimately acting on behalf of MI5 and it is highly unlikely that a public inquest will be held into Peter Wilson's unfortunate death. For security reasons, we feel that any inquest would have to be held in camera. The Wilson family should be informed of what happened, but, because of perceived unlawful entry to Scargill Cottage, with a weapon, we do not believe that any prosecution of Jonathan Maxim for manslaughter could be successfully brought. As for Mrs Law, aka the wife of Michael Maxim, there is proof of her firing a gun at Mr Tanner, whose version of events we fully support. Do you have any other points, Superintendent?'

Blair continued in a straightforward manner.

'Regarding the apprehension of Jonathan Maxim and Mrs Henshaw, how are matters proceeding?'

'Our main concern,' said Dawson, 'is Jonathan Maxim's possible danger to the public. He is being sought, as you know, through the usual police channels, both here and abroad, but we don't feel prosecution would be appropriate, bearing in mind his diagnosed schizophrenia.

Better that he be confined on medical grounds. As for Mrs Henshaw? Yes, she did aid her father and brother but her appearance in a public court, for perverting the course of justice, might be thought to be not in the national interest. And, can I say, before you give me your own views, Superintendent, that the Chief Constable and the Minister do concur with the views I have expressed to you and DI Tate.'

'And what about Mr Tom Henshaw? Assaulted by Mr Tanner, unconscious, hospitalized. An innocent in all this.'

'Well, you say that, but do we really believe that he had no knowledge of the Maxims at Scargill Cottage?'

'My view is that the man is totally innocent!' exclaimed Blair. Dawson glanced at Tanner.

'You are probably correct, Superintendent, but I couldn't take that chance,' offered Tanner.

'If you ask me,' interjected DI Tate, 'this whole mess is your fault. I don't believe for a minute that MI5 sanctioned all this. You'd been put behind a desk in Catterick according to what I heard, and Peter Wilson had retired. He'd never been in the field and hardly knew one end of a gun from another! Where did he get the gun, David? Yours?'

Dawson held his right hand in the air to silence Tanner before he had chance to reply.

'Enough, Alan,' said Blair sternly, 'this will get us nowhere.'

'I know, sir, but I'm the one who'll have to talk to the Wilsons, and Tom Henshaw.'

With that, DI Tate stood up and was gone from the room, slamming the door behind him. Seconds went by before anyone spoke.

'If I was you,' Blair said to Dawson, 'I would consider some form of apology or compensation to Tom Henshaw. A good lawyer would see Mr Tanner in court over this.'

'You may be right,' said Dawson, thoughtfully. 'Perhaps it would help if we got his wife back to him.'

'Good luck with that! And one more thing,' continued Blair, 'I understand that two of your secretives turned up here late, the night before last, with a van and a high-up order, to take away all Jonathan Maxim's computer gear. We do have computer forensics specialists, you know.'

'Yes, Superintendent, but MI5 and GCHQ have the best in the world.'

'And may I ask what you've discovered so far? Any clues to where Maxim and his sister have run to? They must have money, lots of money. After all, they donated a two-million-pound gold treasure to Iraq. Can't you follow the money trail?'

Dawson and Tanner glanced at each other.

'Oh, dear,' said Blair. 'You see, I think we've always been behind the curve with Jonathan Maxim. At times it seems as if he's been playing games, toying with his adversary. I'm going to guess that your world class forensics team have managed to find out bugger all!'

'I think our meeting is at an end, Superintendent Blair. Let me thank you for your cooperation.'

'My pleasure!'

That was the last time that Blair or Tate had any direct contact with MI5 about the Peter Wilson case.

TUESDAY FINAL WEEK IN JULY

The Isle of Man had entered the lives of Jonathan and Sally Maxim twenty-five years before, when Michael Maxim, then a serving SAS officer, had finally persuaded his wife to seek help for her prolonged post-natal depression. She had taken the children to Douglas for three months, not only for an extended holiday, but also to consult a psychiatrist privately. She had improved markedly under therapy, but the psychiatrist had made her aware that her underlying problem was mild schizophrenia, a condition that can be caused by both environmental and genetic factors.

Jonathan started to present symptoms in early teenage, around the same time that his academic brilliance was being recognized. Treatment by cognitive behavioural therapy was extremely successful, but, a few years later, the stresses of life at Cambridge, not being able to fit in, led to a relapse and Jonathan quit the university after two years. He received treatment at a clinic in London, but his delusions and hallucinations continued to increase to the extent that he was put on permanent antipsychotic drugs. At no stage had he shown any tendency to violence. All that changed when his father took him away from treatment, at the age of twenty, not being able to face up to the fact that his own son had mental problems. Jonathan had always looked up to his SAS father, who, now working alongside the Security Service, cynically trained his son in his own image. For the next three years he only had intermittent contact with his mother and sister and did his father's bidding. Then, on that fateful day when two MI5 officers were killed, Michael Maxim had insisted that his own daughter drive him and Jonathan to the safe house, knowing full well what the likely outcome would be. After killing the two officers, Michael Maxim had ensured that his beautiful intelligent daughter was now enmeshed within his world. He used his wife and Sally to engineer his disappearance into Wharfedale, funded not only by the fruits of his own violence but also by his son's increasing brilliance at playing the financial markets. With Jonathan's expertise in digital technology, that would now be exploited in secret in an out-of-the-way cottage in Wharfedale. His future was assured, until that drunken night when Michael Maxim's violence finally caught up with him.

After Michael Maxim's death, life at Scargill Cottage had been peaceful and stable, with Sally very much the head of the household, taking care of her mother and brother, but she had felt increasingly trapped there. She had only bought The Inn to give herself purpose but then fell head over heels. Jonathan's behaviour began to change after she married and moved into the pub. There were days when he failed to take his medication and, over time, delusions returned, not helped by his mother's own mental frailty. The frequency of his mimicking his mother's voice, her look, her manner, had increased markedly in the past year and he had spent more and more days dressed in women's clothing. Nevertheless, he had shown no signs of violence since the patricide, until Peter Wilson walked into the cottage with an automatic pistol in his pocket and recognized him from the student photograph on his mobile phone. As the net had tightened, Sally realized that they must escape from Wharfedale. In the last four years, she had done many runs over to Douglas, banking her father's ill-gotten cash, bit by bit, and had bought a bolt hole just in case. She knew the island well from childhood holidays and Jonny's expertise had amassed over one million pounds, including offshore funds there. The plan had always been to flee to the Isle of Man if needs must. What she hadn't bargained for since setting everything up in Wharfedale, including the purchase of The Inn, which had given her respectability and ordinariness as a local landlady, was falling in love with a very ordinary Yorkshireman, a reliable good man, Tom Henshaw.

On the Tuesday morning after the frosty encounter between Skipton police and MI5, David Tanner knocked on the door of The Inn and stepped back rapidly to a safe distance. Tom Henshaw opened the door and stared at him.

'You've got a nerve,' he said. 'My solicitor's getting in touch with your lot, and the police. You can't go around knocking people out and abducting my wife, no matter who you think you are!'

Tanner held up both palms, trying to placate the landlord.

'You're right, Mr Henshaw. I'm here to apologise and explain and, hopefully, give you good news.'

Tom shook his head in disbelief, but then trundled back in to the bar. Tanner followed. The two men sat opposite each other, both with their arms safely folded. Tanner tried to convince Tom that he had feared for his own life and had, mistakenly, thought that Tom was involved in the whole business up at Scargill Cottage. The landlord didn't believe a word.

'I had no idea Sal had a brother, let alone up there at the cottage. And I'd only seen her mother half a dozen times since our wedding. All a bloody mystery to me. Makes me look daft I suppose, but I love the woman.'

He was desperate not to cry.

'Mr Henshaw, we did have our suspicions of you, but we now know that we were wrong. We don't want this to end up in court, naturally, and I've been given licence to offer you compensation of ten thousand pounds if you agree to taking the matter no further.'

'You know where you can stick your money!' spat out the angry landlord.

'I understand your anger, but there is something else of much greater importance, I'm sure you'll agree.'

'And what's that!'

'Your wife, Sally.'

'What do you mean?' asked Tom, softening his voice.

'She is certainly guilty of perverting the course of justice, after the death of Peter Wilson, and of aiding and abetting her brother, and her father, a known killer. All this we can prove, but all charges will be dropped if you agree to take no action.'

'Can you do that? What about the police? They're after Sal and her brother.'

'This has been looked at by the Security Service at the highest level. Jonathan Maxim is not part of our deal. He is still a wanted man. However, your wife would not be prosecuted and would be free to return to you if you agree. All this can be placed in writing with your solicitor.'

Tom Henshaw did not need any time to consider.

'I probably still hate your guts, Mr Tanner, but of course I'll agree. I just hope she'll come back to me.'

'Do you know where she's gone?' asked Tanner.

'I'm not that stupid, Mr Tanner. It's time you left.'

Tom Henshaw did not move. Tanner nodded respectfully, stood up and walked out of the pub. As he got back into his car, he hoped it would only be a few hours to wait, if that. The phone tap was in place, whether the call was by landline or mobile.

The next morning Tanner rang a London number. He was given details of a landline call placed by Tom Henshaw at 6 p.m. the previous day. It had been to Fred Denby at Scargill Farm, asking him to keep an eye out for the cottage, with no-one now living there. Unknown to Tanner, Tom Henshaw had no way of contacting his wife. He too was waiting.

FINAL WEEK IN AUGUST

Weeks passed with police first concentrating on Carlisle, where Fred Denby's car was discovered. They soon identified the hotel that the two had used but, even with the vast amount of CCTV footage that was examined in detail, neither Sally Henshaw nor Jonathan Maxim could be pinpointed leaving by train. Possible destinations by rail or road, such as London, Newcastle, Glasgow, Edinburgh and Stranraer, were all checked out thoroughly, but the reluctance of the Crown Prosecution Service to commit to prosecution for murder or manslaughter meant that the investigation was both time-limited and under-resourced.

As summer was ending, Sally Henshaw felt more secure. She and her brother were living in a nicely appointed house in Laxey, a few miles outside Douglas, with awe inspiring sea views. Jonny was happy enough. He had his new laptop and could indulge himself with money making on the markets and with playing chess. His expertise and self-confidence meant that discovery online held no fears. For his sister, one worrying aspect was that he now spent most of the day in women's clothing, affecting his mother's voice. Only when admonished by her did he petulantly return to his true self. New identities had been set up for the two of them and Mr and Mrs Barker were welcomed at Island Investments Inc where, as a high net worth investor, Sally was treated with great courtesy by eager financial advisers. Her one big problem was how much she missed Tom. He wasn't a bright man, not particularly handsome, not great at conversation, unable to handle money, and not good at looking after himself. It had baffled her now for over three years, the longing for his touch, the need to take care of him, and the need to be taken care of by him. One August day she went to Laxey station and bought a postcard. On the back of it she wrote a date and a time and a large letter S. On the front, she put a cross. She placed it in an envelope and posted it. Three days later, Tom Henshaw opened the envelope and cried as he examined the postcard.

It was very early in the morning, on the last Thursday in August, when Tom Henshaw set off on the fifty-mile journey to Heysham. Well before eight o'clock, the landrover was in the queue for the ferry crossing to Douglas. On board he sat gazing out to sea. He'd managed to put the horrific events of the past seven weeks out of his mind but, along with elation at the prospect of seeing Sally again, there was fear, fear about Jonathan, that in the end, she might choose her brother over him. She could be free, but Jonny could not. He had never met her brother and there was physical fear too for his own safety. From everything he'd read in newspapers, or been told by the police, Jonathan Maxim could kill.

Tom ate a hearty breakfast before disembarking after the four-hour crossing. He'd never been to the Isle of Man and, as he drove at snail's pace around the busy picturesque bay in Douglas, avoiding the horse-drawn trams full of tourist families, he consulted his satnav. He was soon climbing the winding road up and over to Laxey where he parked in the car park below the towering Wheel. There were dozens of tourists milling about, taking selfies. Sally's postcard had been a photograph of an electric tram at the summit of Snaefell, Man's highest peak. He walked the few hundred yards to the station where he bought himself a ticket and climbed aboard the blue and white Victorian tram with its polished wood window frames. The climb was about five miles, starting in glorious sunshine but today ending at over two thousand feet in mist. On the way up, as the tram crossed the road where TT bikes hurtle past at lunatic speeds, he failed to notice two cars parked on their own in a stoney car park next to The Bungalow. The tram struggled its way to the summit some five hundred feet higher and came to a halt.

'Forty-five minutes 'til the last tram down,' warned the conductor.

As he climbed down from the tram Tom Henshaw stared ahead. Outside the café there were several picnic tables. Seated at the furthest table there were two women. One turned her head towards him. It was a beautiful woman with jet black hair. It was Sally. She stood up and slowly walked towards him, arms outstretched. Surprising himself, the Yorkshireman ran to her and clasped her to his chest, kissing her violently on her scarlet lips.

'I hate your hair,' he said incongruously.

She laughed and they walked into the café. She bought coffees and biscuits and they sat smiling at each other, talking about nothing of importance, just delighting in being together again. They held hands across the table. She smiled for the hundredth time and glanced over her husband's shoulder.

'Hello, Mrs Henshaw, I'm pleased to see you again.'

It was David Tanner. Tom's head spun round but he remained where he was, dumbstruck.

'Hello, Mr Tanner, I half expected to see you. I knew you'd figure out that the only way to get to me and Jonny was through Tom. He's a darling man but easy to follow I suspect.'

She mouthed a kiss to her husband.

'I'm sorry, Sal,' said Tom. 'I promise you I didn't know I was being followed. But they're not going to prosecute you. I've done a deal. It's all in writing. You're free, Sal, free to come home.'

Sally looked angry, but with Tanner, not Tom.

'Free, eh! This man killed my mother in front of my own eyes. And what do you think they're going to do with my brother? Jonny's no killer really, he just thinks he is. He was trained to kill by a madman, but underneath, he's a child. He's no murderer, Mr Tanner!'

175

'He does a good impression of being one,' offered Tanner, sarcastically, still feeling the effects of a knife in the back.

'So why are you here, Mr Tanner? Kill or cure?'

'Not to kill, Mrs Henshaw.'

'Then put the gun that I know you must have, put it down on the table.'

'It stays in my shoulder holster,' he replied. 'Regulations.'

'Then mine will stay in my bag,' she assured him.

He smiled.

'Ah, my automatic I assume, from the cottage. I wondered who had it, you or your brother.'

She nodded.

'Is that Jonny, outside, at the picnic table you were sitting at?'

She nodded again.

'I'm taking a big risk, Mrs Henshaw, being up here on my own, with no backup, partly, maybe, because I feel some sort of guilt at what's happened. Peter Wilson was a friend of mine who posed no threat to your brother. He was just a desk job man, just helping me.'

'Then he shouldn't have been carrying a gun,' she countered.

'True, that was my fault, but we were after Michael Maxim. You know that your father killed two of my colleagues. He also killed a Garda officer over in Ireland. He had to be stopped. The crazy irony in all this is that we were searching for him long after he was dead.'

'I only half believe what you say, Mr Tanner. You would have killed Jonny at the safe house, given the chance.'

Tanner didn't blink, he didn't change expression. There was no tell-tale swallowing or give-away body language.

'The truth is that the safe house operation was botched, and what happened at the cottage should never have happened. Peter Wilson was too brave for his own good. Believe me, I intended, and I still intend, to take Jonathan in alive. You know that he needs treatment. Is he himself today, or is he his mother? And tomorrow? The day after? You must help me.'

She sighed and looked into Tom's pleading eyes. He nodded and reached across the table to hold her hand.

'Jonny hates you, Mr Tanner. He swore that he'd kill you if he ever saw you again. If you go out there, don't touch that gun of yours. You'd be dead in a second. I'm not going to do this for you. I couldn't look Jonny in the face with you at my side. He'd think I'd betrayed him.'

A voice shouted, 'Last tram back down to Laxey, leaving now' and the café and terrace outside quickly emptied, leaving only a young woman in a black summer dress

177

seated at a picnic table. David Tanner walked towards the doorway, leaving Tom and Sally at the table, gripping each other's hands, and stepped out into dazzling sunshine. The mist had gone. He blinked and his vision cleared to reveal Jonathan Maxim standing twenty feet in front of him, smiling and tapping the double-edged blade of his knife on the palm of his left hand, holding it securely in his right. Tanner stopped and held up empty palms.

'We meet again, MI5,' said Maxim in his mother's voice. The likeness was unnerving to Tanner.

'Are you here to kill me? You've failed twice! You only managed to kill mother, but mother's here now, ready to kill you.'

'You are Jonathan Maxim,' stated Tanner. 'You are not a killer! You know that you are not a killer! It is over, Jonathan. I am here to help you.'

Maxim tapped the knife on his left palm with increasing speed.

'And we need you to help us too, Jonathan?'

Maxim stopped the tapping.

'What do you mean?'

'You play your games so well. You led us a merry dance. We need your help.'

'What do you mean?' he asked again.

'We took all your computers away and gave them to our best experts. They tried to find out about all you do online. How you can hide everything, make it invisible, even to them. The way you can make money, the way you can move it about and hide it, everything. They've figured out nothing, Jonathan, absolutely nothing! They can't work out how you do it. They are so impressed, but you've frightened them. What if someone else could do what you can? They need you to work for us.'

Jonathan Maxim burst out laughing.

'It's all a game, Mr Tanner, just a game. It's just fun. It's always been easy, ever since I was ten. Easy.'

It was Jonny's own voice. His mother had gone.

'Can you teach us, Jonathan?'

'For the right price,' he replied, suddenly hurtling his knife with ultimate precision into the ground between Tanner's feet. Tanner did not move.

'Eh, Sal, come out here,' he shouted, 'MI5 wants me to work for him.'

Sally and Tom walked out onto the terrace.

'Oh, that's marvellous, gorgeous boy,' she said softly as she walked to him, tears forming rivulets over her perfect face as she took his hand.

The brother and sister, born only five minutes apart, set off on the path back down the mountain, followed by David Tanner and Tom Henshaw. A few hundred feet lower, at The Bungalow car park, two vehicles were waiting for them, one with armed MI5 officers inside, and one with a psychiatrist and nurse. As the four approached, Tanner raised his right hand high in the air. The doctor and nurse got out of their car, the MI5 officers did not.

As the cars pulled away, David Tanner tapped his shoulder holster, removed his mobile phone from his jacket pocket and held it to his ear.

'Yes, sir, all went to plan, at last.'

'Well done, David,' said Dawson, 'I'll see you in my office, nine o'clock on Monday.'

'Yes, sir.'

Tanner stared skyward.

SIX MONTHS LATER

Back in Skipton, the dust had settled. The death of Peter Wilson had faded into the background, even for the Wilson family itself, and, for the police, Wharfedale was sleepy again. For a time, Scargill Cottage had been a ghoulish diversion on the Triangle Walk, but Fred Denby had put up makeshift 'No Walkers Keep Out' signs and had deterred nosey tourists with his shotgun. By the time winter arrived, normality had returned to Buckden, Hubberholme and Cray.

One mild day in February, PC Mark Craven decided to have a run up to Buckden to see how Mr and Mrs Henshaw were getting on. He liked the Yorkshireman and the contrast between him and his glamourous wife.

He sat chatting to them both for over half an hour in the bar of The Inn and was pleased at their normality. As he got up to get back to his duties, he said:

'Oh, I hear Fred Denby's been looking after Scargill Cottage for you, for money no doubt. He's a bit of a rascal. I hope you don't mind me asking, but are you going to sell it, after all that's happened?'

'No,' said Tom, 'there's someone living up there now.'

'Oh, who?' asked the young police constable.

'My sister,' came the reply.

Craven nodded, turned, and wished them well as he walked out of the pub.

Printed in Poland
by Amazon Fulfillment
Poland Sp. z o.o., Wrocław

49340348R00110